The
UNEXPECTED
Love
Stripper

DANIEL OHALE MADUABUCHI

Order this book online at www.trafford.com
or email orders@trafford.com

Most Trafford titles are also available at major online book retailers.

Printed in the United States of America.

ISBN: 978-1-4669-3931-8 (sc)
ISBN: 978-1-4669-3930-1 (e)

Trafford rev. 05/31/2012

 www.trafford.com

North America & International
toll-free: 1 888 232 4444 (USA & Canada)
phone: 250 383 6864 ♦ fax: 812 355 4082

CONTENTS

Have you ever travelled to a land where you don't even understand their language of communication and all you can understand is the language of love and sacrifices, which you never planned to implant? But the sacrifice you make pulls a great impact on people's lives, then you begin to consider life to be a mystery because you don't know what comes next, whom you are going to love or hate no matter your personality. These may be the reasons why sometimes people can adjust to any condition and bring their personality down to the lowest to achieve that goal that they had aimed.

For my Ukrainian and Russian Friends

Her Motives

Here comes a priceless princess stripping. Her moves are like that of an angel, the way she swims in the air, her body as clean as a white cloud. She smells like a morning rose and shines like a mirror reflecting the sunlight, and her smiles could bring healing to the sick, oh! What a pretty being she is that her motives are perfect and predictable. She moves her body, nicely and slowly winding. She twists her waist in such a way that no man can resist her sexual seduction. Here she comes—the princess of all strippers.

Review

Life can be tragic and, at the same time, mysterious. Some people can do everything possible to make sure that their children get the best in life. They don't even care about other people's children, whom they abuse and molest in order to make fortune. That is why, when life becomes a tragedy for them, no one cares.

Have you ever travelled to a land where you don't even understand their language of communication and all you can understand is the language of love and sacrifices, which you never planned to implant? But the sacrifice you make pulls a great impact on people's lives, then you begin to consider life to be a mystery because you don't know what comes next, whom you are going to love or hate no matter your personality. These may be the reasons why sometimes people can adjust to any condition and bring their personality down to the lowest to achieve that goal that they had aimed.

More than 30 percent of the world's population lives on bondage directly or indirectly. Some of these bondages could be hidden "indirectly," which cause havoc, pains, and sufferings in the hearts of men, while some are—as a result of having no choice left—for a particular occupation or career in life that are broadly seen "directly." So it's our right to help these people that are captured in bondage, whether directly or indirectly.

Natasha's life has been a tragedy. She doesn't know where to begin. It all happened like a dream; it was so fast that she can barely remember it all. She woke up one morning and saw herself in an environment made up of beautiful young girls like her, and in a short while, she only discovered that there was no way out and nowhere to run. Though life in there was quite better and interesting, she sought for freedom.

The Unexpected Love is a story of beautiful young lady, Natasha, from the Russian Federation, whose freedom is confined within an environment. Natasha stripteases in a well-known Entertainment company in such a way that no man can escape her sexual seduction. Many Mafia members pay a lot of money to see her strip. She makes lots of money to the company, and the company does everything possible to maintain and to retain her.

A young black American tourist, Fred Smith, has an opportunity to watch Natasha strip. At first sight, he falls in love with her and wants to do everything possible to get her out of her bondage, which is a difficult task for him. At the cost of getting his love out of bondage, there is so much bloodshed as he clashes with the Mafia, who owns the company who will never let Natasha go.

CHAPTER ONE

The Tune

*T*he tune of the music so melodious!

Pleasing to listen!

It fills the ears of the desired with passion and exertion!

The sound sweeps through the surroundings, echoing in and out!

Bringing out smiles from the faces of its listeners!

The ears are so large and eager to listen to the music again and again!

The beat of the sound is so strong that it can pass through the walls so softly and raise the souls that are asleep!

It brings joy and happiness, welcoming the audience!

The wave of the sounds shakes the heart with a higher frequency!

The body is put into vibration!

Bringing out some eagerness!

This eagerness triggers enthusiasm!

Making everyone to feel a ray!

The eyes of the viewers never wish to be closed!

The strippers dance to the tune of techno, which is their favorite tune.

It is amazing and colorful, the way the strippers dance. They move their bodies up and down, stripping to seduce their audience.

The strippers are professional erotic dancers. They perform contemporary forms of striptease. Unlike in burlesque, the performer in the modern form of stripping minimizes the interaction of customer and dancer, reducing the importance of tease in the performance in favor of speed to undress. Not every stripper will end her performance completely nude, though full nudity is common where not prohibited by law. The integration of the stripper pole as a nearly ubiquitous prop has also shifted the emphasis in the performance toward a more acrobatic, explicit expression versus the slow-developing burlesque.

The strippers wear very sexy short, skinny skirts that almost expose their panties. The bright bras they wear can't cover their bosoms properly. They are so loose that they create more attraction. Men focus on them, waiting for them to striptease. The strippers dance smoothly on their high-heeled shoes without even being wired about it.

The music doesn't stop getting more interesting. The rhythm rhymes with the lyrics. Men toast and keep ordering for more drinks.

As the strippers dance, their bodies reflect the sparkling light. Men see them as fire from a furnace. Their beauties are beyond compare. A diamond stud is pierced on the left side of their noses and on their bellies. It gives them an amazing appearance. The tribal tattoo on their lower backs and the silver ring on their right thumbs create a lot of attraction. The strippers toned, and every eye that watches them wishes to have them for the night at least once in their lifetime!

The more the clock ticks, the more men of caliber keep entering the club, making impressions on the audience. The beat of the music keeps pumping to the walls, echoing! Alas! No one can escape the tune of the music as everyone keeps being happy, shouting to the air. The big guys who can't dance keep on nodding their heads up and down to the melodious tune. It is a casual night club named Fun Club, where everything is provided with no specialty. Fun Club is divided into two parts. The upper part is basically made for the VIPs, and the lower part is for the casual audience, though the dance floor is located in lower part, so the VIPs still walk down to the dance floor to dance. So it does not really make much difference. It's just the pattern of the design that makes the difference. Fun Club comprises of everything in a big furnished hall. Set fixtures, a luxurious mix of crystals, Pucci fabrics, baby croc and leather, a futuristic glass fireplace, vacuum-compressed elevators, electric Tinseltown-era artifacts, and ebony Macassar—creating a vibe that gives a modern feel. A long ground bar with a stylish design of a series of drinks, the stripper's stage directly facing the main dance flow, well-decorated resting leather seats, and crystal red wall papers—Fun Club is decorated in such a way that when people come in, most people inside notice their presence.

It's about 12:30 a.m. when Fred Smith and James Johnson walk into Fun Club with their American looks. I mean their appearance is so cute and unique from every other man in the club. Many eyes are on them because of the indifference as the steward matches them up to a free reserved seat where they settle down. The people around them easily notice that they are black Americans—definitely from their looks, skin color, voice intonation, behavior, and mood. Some people around still wonder the reason why they chose to be in Fun Club. It's rare to see their personality in Fun Club, which is mostly made for the "less privileged" they said. Soon, the DJ also notices their presence as he plays an English song, which keeps them relieved.

"I love this place. It's making lot of sense. At least they're playing an English song, not only those Russian songs, though I love the beats and their crazy dance," said Fred.

"Come on, we just checked in. I told you it's gonna be fun. The club is just starting," said James smiling.

"You don't get me, man. Look at that steward, I mean the girl that walked us up to this seat. Can you see how pretty and hot she is?" asked Fred.

"Oh! Dude, you have started again! Come on, every girl here in the Russian Federation, especially here in Ukraine, seems to be pretty, easy, innocent, and they are all attractive," James replied to Fred, and as they were still speaking, another steward, more sexily dressed, walked up to them.

"Good evening, gentlemen." She kept smiling. "Here is the menu. What do you desire for? Or what can I get for you?" questioned steward 2.

"Holy Mary mother of God, you must be kidding me. I like the impression here. I was just thinking of how I'm going speak this funny, difficult Russian language, and here she comes saving my ass. Gosh, I'm sorry, young lady! How do you know that we don't speak the Russian language? The few people we've met who understood English still pretend as if they don't know it. Maybe they are shy. I just don't know. So what's up with you? What gave you the hint?" Fred asked.

"It's our service, sir. From people's moods, we can tell the part of the world they belong to," said steward 2.

"We know that of course. I mean the intonation, the accent, where did it come from? How do you know we are damn Americans? How many times have you been to United States? Your intonation is a remarkable one, but I know you are a Ukrainian girl," expressed James.

Steward 2, laughing and blushing, said, "It's also our service. We are taught on how to address people from different parts of the world. It's my job." She kept smiling and said, "Gentlemen, I guess I have to go now. My time is up with you. I must attend to other customers. In a short while, someone will come and get you guys what you choose to drink or eat." As she slowly walked away, Fred tried to pull her back by telling her some funny stuff, but she resisted and kept smiling, waved good-bye, and also pointed at her watch for him, meaning time's up. Fred was very surprised at the way things were done and organized in the fun club. It was unusual from the previous places they visited.

I can't still understand why every girl stirs at us. Even the stewards are all charming. They look like angels. They are sexily dressed like porn nurses! I'm so relieved. Speaking with a girl that understands the language that I speak, I feel like speaking with her forever. It's so interesting. I don't have to start stressing my brain, thinking of what shit that I'm going to say," said Fred.

"You're right. First impression really matters a lot. This place seems to be cool compared to other cafes and clubs we've been to in this country. This night is really gonna be so hot. We are going to feel at home. We are going to feel a modern environment again." As James was speaking, Fred was busy going through the pages of the menu without understanding anything. Suddenly, steward 3 interrupted, speaking to them in the Russian language.

"Hello, gentlemen, I guessed you might need my help," said steward 3.

Fred cried out loud while looking at her beauty, "Come on, this can't be happening again. We thought we're in the right place to feel at home, speaking to people who understand us. Please, we do not speak Russian." He demonstrated with his hand, saying, "Russian no." Steward 3 laughed.

"I'm so sorry. I was kidding," she replied in the English language, and James breathed out so heavily with relief. "So, gentlemen, what do you really want? My work is to interpret the menu for foreigners." She explained every part of the pages of the menu to them, and they order a bottle of Hennessy, which seemed to be one of the most expensive drinks in the menu. Steward 3 is quite surprised when they demand for a full bottle of Hennessey. It's unusual for just two guys to demand for 1.5 liters of Hennessey. How are they going to finish it? (Steward 3's English isn't as strong as steward 2's. She spoke so gently like a normal Russian who learned English, I mean picking the words one after the other.)

Fun Club was getting more filled up, and the music kept pumping out endlessly, giving men more reasons to drink. Fred and James were sipping on their Hennessey, jesting about the way girls stared at them, which was unusual in the United States. Maybe because they were foreigners. Within a short while, three pretty girls that seemed matured, buoyant, and decently dressed danced up to their seats and kept dancing in front of them. It was quite interesting and amazing as they twisted their waists up and down, dancing to the tune of the music and also giving them eyes of notice. Immediately, the song that was playing stopped. The three young ladies rushed up to them, introducing themselves. The first introduced herself as Inna; the second, Elena; and the third, Tanya. Fred and James, who knew little Russian, said the few words they understand in Russian. And the girls also spoke little English they understand. It was really fun as they used eyes and hands to communicate with one another. The girls were so eager to be with them because of their swag and indifference. James and Fred were now pretty tipsy. They understood that the girls wanted to drink together and have fun with them, which was a normal thing for girls in the club. Fred called steward 3 to find out what the girls wanted to drink, but surprisingly, they said "Anything." Fred then demanded for a bottle of Baileys and Ukraine vodka, suggested by the steward. James presented the drink to them, and they appreciated it and they toasted to friendship and more fun. It was quite confusing to Fred and James to make the choice on whom to go home with for the night. There were three girls, and they all seemed so pretty and accommodating, but Fred would not stop admiring steward 2, Kata. Soon one of the girls, Elena, walked up to the DJ and whispered something in his ears. I guess she told him to play one of her favorite English love songs. When this love song was played, she persuaded Fred to dance with her. Fred was left with no choice. He stood up and started rocking to the song with her. Soon James stood up with Inna, and they also started dancing to the tune of sweet jazz, slowly and step by step. The pattern and the way they uniformly danced were cool and entertaining. People around kept admiring them, more especially the girls that wished they were the ones dancing with these humble gentlemen, who were entirely different from their Ukrainian men, whom the girls thought didn't know how to rock jazz in the rightful way. After the little dance, they sat down and took a nap, and the girls excused themselves to go to the ladies' room. Maybe they wanted to speak to themselves alone because Tanya was pretty sad. She was the one who pushed her friends out in order to chill with the foreigners, and now she was left alone.

Fred took a walk to the bar at the lower floor to see a pretty girl he sighted and so much admired. As he walked down the staircase, eyes were on him. His unique attire created more attraction. The way he stylishly walked, made him the real man of the night "girls whispered". Upon getting to the bar, he sat down close to the girl and demanded for two shots of whisky. He presented one to her, and they toasted.

"Señorita! You look too beautiful." The pretty girl, who seemed not to understand him very well just smile. Off course every other language understands the word "beautiful" in English language. Fred tried to speak with her but she could hardly understand him. Fred coded and immediately greeted her in the Russian language. "Hi, beautiful girl. I'm Smith! What is your name?" he asked. She now replied, smiling, "My name is Tatiana."

Tatiana was happy to introduce herself to him, and she asked him the usual question everyone here, especially girls, seemed to ask every foreigner.

"What country do you come from, and what has brought you to my country?" she asked.

"I'm from the United States, Los Angeles. I'm here for my summer fun. I needed to experience something different," said Fred. When Tatiana heard that he was from the United States, she was surprised and excited. She became more interested in knowing him better because the Americans rarely came to Ukraine. She thought, And even though they do, they would be hardly seen. "I like America. Would you take me there with you?" She smiled. "How long have you been staying in Ukraine? I like the way you speak Russian. It's interesting, and you are sweet." Fred smiled back at her, looked into her blue eyes, stared at her bosom as well, and replied, "I have been staying here for almost a week, and it has really been fun." Fred answered these questions so accurately in the Russian language due to the fact that whenever he was tipsy, he remembered things so easily, and it was also one of the major questions that people there asked. And moreover, he was a quick leaner. Their discussion was becoming more interesting, but unfortunately for Fred, a guy who had less swag and worth not to be inside the club—as graded by Fred—just walked up to Tatiana and started kissing her with passion in Fred's presence. Fred was totally disappointed as she left with him, waving good-bye, smiling. Fred was pissed off for such a shame—a sweet girl, well dressed and fashionable, with a drunken-smelling, dirty guy. "This guy is not worth such a pretty girl at all."

Fred sighed and demands for another shot of whisky. A guy came by and said hey to him. "Hi, my name is Bogdan. I guess you are new here. I'm from Germany," he expressed himself. "I'm Fred from Los Angelis, California," Fred replied. They shook hands and toasted. Bogdan spoke quite understandable English. "What has brought you to our city? Hope you are not a government agent or spy," Bogdan asked. Fred smiled and replied, "Hmm! I'm not. Even if I am, then what? You won't be sitting here with me, sipping on alcohol, and allowing these bitches to stare at you." They both smiled and took a toast for another shout. "How do you find this place? I mean BerryX club. Hope you are feeling good," Bogdan asked.

"Hmm! Quite good. At least I'm having fun. I think I like this place." He smiled. A girl walked toward him and danced in front of him, giving him some signs of interest. "Every girl seems to like you, so which of them are you taking home tonight?" asked Bogdan.

"It's a difficult question. I don't know. There are many girls, and I'm at a loss on choices. What about you?" said Fred.

"They are all our girls," "said Bogdan smiling. "I go home with any girl I wish to go home with no matter her specialty, except for the girls who work here."

"What do you mean by 'except the girls who works here'? Aren't they meant to be easier?" asked Fred, smiling at Bogdan.

"They seem to be the prettiest girls in the city and good enough to have for the night, but their protocols are too much for the ordinary men," said Bogdan.

"What protocol?" Fred asked.

"My friend, you are a stranger here, so you won't understand what I'm talking about. This is the most amazing club in the city. Everything you want, you will find it in this club, BerryX." Bogdan stretched. Fred looked a little bit confused and tipsy. He tried to figure out what Bogdan meant by "Everything one needs, he will find in this club."

"But the club is not all that big. Man, you are damned. Tell me more about this club. I have read little about it, but what I expected is not what I have seen. I have expected more." Fred was still speaking when James texted him through Phone chat. It read, "Where are you, homie? I'm already doing the stuff with Inna, the blond girl, in the toilet. She's wet and tight." James attached a picture of Inna's ass to the message. When Fred read this message, he smiled and wondered when James would stop being rude.

"My friend, I will tell you more about BerryX. Let's take another shot of whisky, then we shall take a walk," said a drunk Bogdan.

"All right, Bogdan." They toasted. A girl walked to Bogdan and whispered in his ears, saying, "I love your friend," but Bogdan kept it to himself. "BerryX is a place made for big guys and big ladies only, wherein the service is the best among all other clubs or cafés in the state, and has become a culture that any able man that has not visited this building, BerryX, has not yet completed his manhood because it's a place for partnership, a place for friendship, and a place for meeting the big guys or the Mafia in the town. It's a home for business discussion and a place for sure and pretty ladies, free of charge, and also for cash," said Bogdan smiling.

Fred smiled back at him and said, "Let's take a walk. I want to see the other parts of this building."

"It's going to cost you some money. I mean very big cash because these places have already been reserved, and I do not plan to visit these places. I hardly go to other parts of the club because of the expenses," said Bogdan.

Fred smiled and said, "Come on, let's go! Money won't be a problem."

Bogdan took his time taking Fred to every part of the club. It seemed as if it were another world entirely. The rooms were all made of crystals and ornaments. Fred wondered how rich the owner of BerryX could be for providing such facilities. In every passage corridor, there was always a receptionist with her computer, communicating and directing guests to their desired location. Not only that, there were also muscular security guards everywhere. Fred wondered if the president was inside the building. Bogdan and Fred visited the casino bar, which was located on the last floor. It was a subparadise designed for the able men. The casino's bar was directly facing a joint called Ambush. It was a place where the Mafia and other prominent men in the state did their meetings and also relaxed. Ambush had a setup with a warm, intimate vibe. The room featured leather and Pucci-fabric seating, a grand bar with a crystal prism, a modern glass-enclosed fireplace, and several plasma screens for video projection and branding, which displays images of the strippers stripping in the club. Every man who entered Ambush was entitled to a free girl of his choice for the night, and the girls were always half-naked. They dressed to kill, even the stewards. Ambush was regarded as the most expensive café in BerryX. Fred wanted to visit Ambush, but Bogdan disagreed because when people who did not belong visit, the Mafia would have eyes on them to find out who they were and what they really wanted, which might be bad. They also went to Ladies' Beach, which was located in the second underground floor. In Ladies' Beach, the ladies alone entertained customers in the swimming pool. Ladies' Beach was a place for casual relaxation for guests who spent the night at BerryX hotel.

The first underground floor was mainly for the strippers. This was the most interesting part of BerryX, where the female strippers displayed their talent in full. Fred was eager to get in because he loved watching girls strip, more especially when he was tipsy.

The strippers' part of the club, a home for pleasure, named Pleasure Paradise, was unique from every other part of the club. It was well refurbished and decorated with different kinds of ornaments that attracted sexual pleasure and comfort. The dramatic design was inspired by the Mafia. It was decorated in a technical way whereby the men sat cubically around a table, as in like a conference table, made up of thick transparent glass divided into chambers. The men sat separately and comfortably on the chairs, which were in alignment with the square transparent table, and the girls stripped linearly along in the middle of the edgeless table, giving them the sensation that they ever urged, a pleasure and a romantic moment of rest. Fred's tipsiness gradually reduced. At their arrival in Pleasure Paradise, he was overwhelmed with the performance. Bogdan's tipsiness seemed to have increased. He sat beside Fred, and Fred ordered for a drink.

The strippers danced in rotation. A set of dancers, in turn, performed for one or more songs in a fixed sequence, which repeated during a shift. Featured entertainers were not usually part of the rotation and had set times when they would perform that were advertised throughout the shift. The DJ emceed the rotation of the strippers and typically announced the current dancers on stage and possibly who to expect in future sets.

It wasn't up to a minute that Fred and Bogdan came into Pleasure Paradise.

Here came a priceless princess stripping.

Her moves were like that of an angel. The way she swam in the air, her body was as clean as a white cloud. She smelled like a morning rose and shone like a mirror reflecting the sunlight, and her smiles could bring healing to the sick, oh! What a pretty being was she that her motives were perfect and predictable. She moved her body, nicely and slowly winding. She twisted her waist in such a way that no man could resist her sexual seduction. Here she came—the princess of all strippers.

Fred was already carried away by this sexy, sweet stripper. He kept on watching her with passion attached on emotion and love. His mind ran through miles in the stripper's body. What a sexual threat. He couldn't control his mind any longer as he concentrated watching her striptease. Bogdan tapped at him. "Smith. Are you all right? I have been calling you, but you never cared to answer.

You just kept on watching Natasha. Come on, let's drink. You can't have her even if you wish."

Fred quickly responded, "Do you know her? Is she Natasha? I mean the other stripper in the middle of the table. The one smiling at us, the tanned skin. She is extremely beautiful. I think she's the most beautiful girl that I have seen this year. I'm really tripping for her." Bogdan smiled. "Moĭ drug." My friend. "She is truly beautiful, and everyone seems to be tripping for her. I have only watched her strip once, and I pissed off spam all over my boxer. I wanted to pay for private stripping, but the money involved is too much just for stripping. She's the best and the prettiest stripper that I have ever seen in my life too. Look at her booms, the way they moves up and down with confidence and perfection. She is the princess of all the strippers in BerryX. According to what I heard and have seen, men pay lots of money to watch her striptease. Take a look at the strippers' list. She's the most expensive. Her price is twice the others. I was wondering why we paid about one hundred US dollars extra for just an entrance fee. I just found out now that it's because Natasha is stripping today. It's so good that I met you today. At least I will remember you for Natasha."

Fred seemed to be confused. He tried so many time to call James to come and see what he was experiencing, but James never answered the calls or even replied to his messages because he was busy dancing with girls in Fun Club. Soon Natasha left her pole and danced close to Fred. Her face was filled with lots of smiles. She stretched her hands, pointing at Fred. Fred was going crazy because the beauty he had seen from afar wasn't as elegant like the one he was seeing right now. She was just like an angel. Her smiles, her breath, and her body were too amazing and so filtered. Fred did not know what to do as she danced away from him to the other edge of the table, where other men were busy placing money on her or tossing it on stage or, more directly, crumpling bills into a ball shape and throwing them in the her direction. Tipping during a stage performance was prohibited due to restrictions in local ordinance or past incidents on the premises, but still there were calibers of personalities that were above the law. Natasha kept on seducing them with her enthusiastic body.

"My friend." Fred called on Bogdan's attention. "What must I do to go home with her tonight?" He pointed at Natasha. "My conscience will never stop threatening me if I don't speak with her tonight."

"I'm sorry, my friend, you can't speak with her for now, and neither can you go home with her tonight no matter how hard you try and the amount of money you may offer. No one is going to listen to you because I know that she has been fully booked by the Mafia for private stripteasing," said Bogdan.

"You mean even when she's through with her stripping today, I can't speak with her? This is insane. You can't tell me that I won't be able to speak with the girl I want. It's impossible. I have the right to speak with any girl I want. I move out with any caliber of women, not even an ordinary club stripper. That is what I'm known for, and that is the reason why I don't fail. That is the reason why I bring my level down to the lowest to achieve what I really want," said Fred.

"Look, my friend, no matter how skillful you are, Natasha is not like any other girl. Clubs don't easily give out their strippers for sex as you know, and now you are talking about the princess that every man wants. Come on, go ahead and try. Talk to the administrators and see what they will say about her," said Bogdan.

"I have spoken with the administrators, but they all pretended as if they don't even understand English. I was shocked," said Fred.

As they were still drinking and speaking, Natasha danced back to their table. Now she was directly facing Fred. She danced slowly, stripteasing. She striped off her bra; her breast was so cute and succulent like a fresh apple. Fred was now tormented as she gradually danced away again. Everyone was amazed with the pattern to which the five strippers stripteased off their bras consecutively in front of any man they wished. Now the stripping seemed to be more interesting to watch. Men became more amazed. Natasha, who seemed to have noticed Fred, the way he looked at her with passion and with a lot of concentration, danced back to him. She kept twisting in his front, slowly winding and bringing out smiles of illusion, and Fred wouldn't stop looking at her with sexual intensions. He felt like grabbing her once and for all. Each time he tried stretching his hands to touch her, he quickly remembered that touching and speaking was highly prohibited in Pleasure Paradise. It was just a sit-and-watch game. Surprisingly, she whispered to his ears, "You're a cute guy." Her accent was so good. Fred smiled, liking her more for the English and developing more interest. Within a short while, the five strippers went off the stage, and another five also showed up immediately. Fred felt disappointed as he watched Natasha leaving the stage, accompanied by some huge men, and she kept waving good-bye to all her fans.

CHAPTER TWO

Hangover

$\mathcal{S}$ometimes in life we find it difficult to differentiate between our dreams and reality. Most times we seem to be confused whether it's happening in the real world or in our dreams. When the world of reality stings and hurts, we only wish it was a dream. To every big guy, there may be something awful about him no matter his level in life, and so it is with girls.

It was about 9:00 a.m. Fred woke up like someone who saw a very bad dream. He jumped off the bed, shocked at seeing himself naked. He wandered around like a lost sheep and immediately put on his boxers. His thoughts were filled with lots of confusion. He started screaming James's name, who was busy with his morning exercises.

Fred walked up to James. "Dude! What happened last night? Why was I naked this morning? What is happening? Oh! Shit! This can't be happening. I never planned to sleep with her so quickly. She is a beautiful girl, isn't she? I mean the girl Natasha."

James paused and started laughing. "Dude, don't tell me that you were that drunk? It's cool to see you in this state for the first time. It's really amazing. Come on, go to the refrigerator and get a cup of water."

"Dude, what are you talking about? I wasn't that drunk! Everything seemed to me like a dream," said Fred.

James was still laughing. "What's up with this girl Natasha that you have been calling all night? It's so strange of you."

"You didn't see the girl I slept with? The pretty angel. I was calling you last night to come and see her strip, but you never answered," said Fred.

James was still laughing. "Yeah, pretty angel? It seemed as if you didn't know the girl that you slept with last night. Just get over it. Go and take a shower to clear your eyes or take a cup of water as I said earlier." James would not stop laughing.

"Please, I'm serious. Tell me. How is she? I mean the stripper," said Fred again, and James paused, laughing, and later on continued smiling. "The girl you slept with, she's Inna, the blond girl that I had sex with in the toilet last night."

Fred was shocked. "What? Come on, you must be kidding me right? I can't make love to the girl that you used. Dude! Stop playing with me simply because I was drunk. I'm not the first person to get drunk, and moreover, when you get drunk, I don't play or make fun of you," Fred complained.

"I'm sorry, dude, but you did sleep with her," said James.

"But why did you let me do that? Weren't there other girls?" asked Fred.

"There were. In fact, excess pretty girls. But you insisted on Inna the blonde because I sent the photo of her ass to you and you kept looking at it while we were still waiting for your limousine cab."

"Come on, dude, what limousine again?" said Fred.

"Don't you remember that you also pasted your friend Bogdan to get a limousine vehicle to take us home? You insisted that you won't go home with other vehicles except a limousine. It was really fun on how serious you were on your drunkenness, but only I knew because you were still strong and speaking with confidence as if you haven't even tasted any alcohol. Everything you said I nearly believed you, but you wouldn't stop kissing all the girls. It wouldn't stop you from the decision you've made to go home with Inna the blonde. When the limousine arrived, some girls came around. They were three beautiful girls, and they wanted to go home with us to continue the fun, but you insisted that you wanted Inna, so I went in search for Inna, and when I saw her, she was happy to follow me. I was with the three girls, and you were with Inna. I wanted to add another girl to you, but you refused and said that you wanted to be with Inna alone, whom you kept calling Natasha. She kept telling you that her name is Inna, not Natasha. It came to an extent that she ignored you and answered Natasha because that's what you kept calling her," said James.

"This is so crazy of me. What was I thinking? Man! That Bogdan of a guy got me so high, and I have pissed myself up. So only you slept with three girls?" complained Fred.

"Oops! You can say that again! It wasn't easy. That was the first time that I slept with three girls at a time. It was really crazy and fun. It seemed as if I was a porn star. But you nearly killed Inna the blonde," said James.

"What are you talking about?" Fred asked James.

"The way you had sex with her like a bitch, hitting her ass and shouting. She was screaming and crying, but you wouldn't let go." James laughed.

"Come on, dude, don't tell lies. I'm not harsh on girls, and I have never been that crazy before," said Fred.

"That wasn't all. The steward had to come and knock on our door several times so that she could reduce her noise because her voice was so loud that other people heard. One of the girls that I was making love with liked the way you had sex and wanted me to have sex with her so hard so that she could also shout, but I can't kill myself and I'm not a porn star. If not for my muscular body, I would have fainted trying to satisfy those little girls. Russian girls are so strong," said James.

"So where are the girls?" Fred asks."

James laughed! "What girls? You still wanna have sex? Come on, dude, Inna left very early this morning when you released her with tears all over her face. She ran for her life. She will never come near us again after what you did to her. You know she's quite a small girl. She just turned eighteen. So for her to experience such hard sex from men like us never tells well. I really felt for her. She had no leg to walk."

"Stop! It's enough. I don't want to hear about this again. I will never get drunk and make love with a girl again that I don't even know. If what you said is true, it's really bad for me. She's eighteen." Fred felt bad.

"Come on, dude, it was cool. It was just that Inna was still a kid. If she was used to sex, she would have enjoyed it. So tell me about this Natasha that has been on your mouth ever since yesterday, or was that imagination or some kind of tipsy stuff?" James asked laughing. Fred was so quiet and calm; soon he started to narrate the story for James, telling him how he felt for her.

"Fred, you again and your fairy tales. Come on, you can't fall in love with that club stripper. You of all people, of all girls you've chosen to fall in love with, a stripper. Well, I know you better than any other person. After you got her in bed, you will let her go as usual, and this time around, she's even a stripper. I remembered last year that was how you forced me to follow you to Spain, where you have seen a girl that you wanna marry simply because she won Miss Spain for that year. We went and spent a lot of money to get her laid, and all of a sudden, you said that she's not your type. Now tell me, how you can fall for a stripper, just a stripper," James spoke with seriousness.

"Johnson, for god's sake, she's the best. You don't know how I feel about her. She has just captivated my heart, and my thoughts, they're all about her. I would have taken pics of her, but cameras are not allowed as usual. You need to see this girl," Fred expressed.

"My eyes open and close, smiles keeps rolling around my feelings!

"Could this be a dream? I never asked for a diamond, but here is gold in my hands!

"I looked at her long hair and how soft it is, like loitering smoke in the sky!

"It's so cute and pleasant holding gold and feeling a nice breath!

"The warmest breath and sensation that could keep you living and loving forever!

"My god, her lips were shining like the morning sun and were succulent like a morning fruit!

"The curve of her lips made me wow and want to kiss her, but this crazy thought kept me real!

"Her pointed nose made her beauty to exclaim and be ultimate among others!

"My imagination began to change but thought it wasn't real!

"Such beauty is a beauty of the fittest in the scene of a deserving prince! And here I am king of the prince." Fred walks around the room, saying all these nice words.

James burst into laughter. "Come on, dude, all these poems are for her! You never told me that you are this good in poetry. So this is what you've being doing to get their hearts. Oh! May God help my friend to get Natasha laid on his bed so that his mind will calm down."

"Johnson, you see your life? You never know when someone is joking or serious. I was really captivated. I mean it," said Fred.

"Let me hear something, please," James complained and continued his press-up exercises and also smiled at Fred. Fred lay on the bed and kept on thinking on how he was going to get Natasha closer to him. Soon he left for a shower.

A female steward came to clean up their apartment. James wouldn't stop looking at her ass, though she was beautiful and also attractive. James kept on speaking with her in the English language, which she never understood. The steward kept on smiling, doing her work. Fred screamed from the bathroom at James, "Can you stop following her all about and let her do her job? Stop saying f-words to her. She doesn't even understand any shit that you are saying. I thought you slept with three girls last night? What's wrong with you?"

"Dude, that was last night, and moreover I have renewed my energy. You better keep shut over there because she's not your type. She's still a little girl like Inna, and I'm just trying to catch fun with her. Moreover, she likes what I'm saying to her. Just allow me to have fun here, because when I get back to the States, I will never have such a time again and I will also not see these people, so get over it," said James.

There was a little silence as the door opened and closed, and Fred reluctantly came out of the bathroom in his little boxers. His towel hung on his neck. He was shocked as the cleaner, whom he thought was staring at him, was smiling, maybe due to his big balls. Fred quickly covered himself with his towel and screamed at James again for not telling him that the girl was still around. "Oops! Dude, it seems she likes you more than me," James said, smiling as usual. "Please be fast and come to the dining table. I am damn hungry."

Fred came for tourism in Ukraine with his Friend James. They heard a lot about the Ukrainian girls—how beautiful, easygoing, and gentle they were. This very hot summer, Fred and Johnson had a long break, so they decided to spend a few weeks here in Ukraine to experience a different environment entirely. In fact, they needed something different. They actually arrived first in a city called Simferopol and headed for Odessa to see the Black

Sea, where they could have fun with girls at the waterside because it was a hot summer.

Fred was a noble, handsome man of about twenty-eight years. He was physically fit, pretty muscular, sexy, and desired by every girl who came his way. His round beard and short hair made him so cute, simple, and responsible. Fred loved his job as a tour guide because it enabled him to travel worldwide and become stronger as he learned other languages. Fred studied international relationships and obtained a master's degree in tourism. His father, George, was a British who had settled down in America and made a lot of money from his international business. He later divorced Fred's mother, Nancy, a black American woman from Louisiana, when Fred was still seventeen. George left a lot of money and property for Fred, and through his connections, Fred has worked in different companies and associations and has made a lot of cash. He was currently working as a senior staff at the US tourism in California. Fred knew how to play his roles when it came to business and work. But it wouldn't stop him from being a womanizer and also a comedian. Fred's father was pure British, but Fred never cared about it. He lived all his life in the States. He has only travelled once to his father's homeland, when he was fifteen. And even up to date, he didn't want to see his father, who was now happily married to a British woman, "his business partner in England."

Fred and James came all the way from the United States of America to the Russian Federation, Ukraine, to have fun this summer 2005. On their arrival, the things they saw around them were fun. The people's way of life, their harsh speech, and everything was just fun. Fred, being a tourist, lowered himself down. He walked on the street; he visited their market places and some tourism centers to make stories with James. They even entered the public bus just for fun. The ancient buildings, routes, and the surroundings were totally different, and they really felt the people's love, care, and jokes. This trip reminded Fred about his three days trip to Poland years back. Poland was more modernized and organized than Ukraine. There are similarities in their life style. Poland would be more socialized. He thought about it but would draw a conclusion after his tour in Ukraine. The Number of girls in Ukraine is unbelievable compared to Poland. Ukraine has a population more of girls. The girls are prettier than Polish girls but not socialized like the Polish girls. English could be the problem *"Fred thought about it"*. Good population of the Polish people understood English Language. It has really made it easier for foreigners. It has also contributed to more growth and development in Poland.

Fred and James arrived at Simferopol airport and proceeded to Odessa, where they lodged in a hotel close to the Black Sea, where they were going to spend the holiday. The next day they walked up to the sea, and it was so amazing over there. The ladies were so sexy, friendly, and beautiful, but the basic problem they had with them was communication. They understood the minor part of the Russian language as tourists. Notwithstanding few girls understood little English Language and it was so cool hanging out with them. At the end of every day, Fred and James went home with different girls for fun. After a few days, they decided to visit other cities in Ukraine, starting with Kiev, the capital. They visited some nightclubs and cafés in Kiev and had lots of fun with girls, and now they were in Donetsk, catching more fun.

James has been a childhood friend to Fred, though he was about two years older than he was and also more muscular and taller. They grew up together as tight friends. They attended the same university, but he studied Journalism. Thus, whenever Fred traveled to any country for tourism, James was always his right-hand man and also his journalist.

CHAPTER THREE

Bogdan and Inna

*B*ogdan was used to drinking and never had hangovers; he woke up strong and normal at the usual time and left for work. Bogdan was a German who had been in Ukraine ever since he was sixteen. He came for studies in Ukraine because his father often came to Ukraine for business purposes and demanded that he should study there, that it would enable him to learn the Russian language better. Bogdan enrolled for his degree, which took him about six years to obtain. He studied international relations and had obtained all the necessary certificates that he needed. He has been working at the German embassy in Ukraine for the past ten years and loved his job because he got a lot time for himself and had also got to know a lot of people here and other parts of the world. He worked as a senior staff in the embassy. It was around 11:30 a.m. when Fred called to find out how Bogdan was doing, only to discover that he was already in his office.

"Fred, hello, my friend, how are you doing?"

"Hope you remember me, Bogdan."

"Yes, of course, my *drug* Smith. How are you doing? It was really fun hanging out with you guest. Hope you had fun with those girls when I left."

Fred said, "Oh yes, we did. It was really a crazy fun. So how are you feeling now? Hope good because yesterday you were a bit higher than me!"

Bogdan, smiling, said, "My friend, I'm doing great. I'm right in my office attending to visitors. Drinking and smoking has been part of me since I was twelve years old, so it's never had much side effect on me. I resumed work by eight a.m. this morning." Fred was shocked, wondering how possible that could be. He was so tipsy last night and went home very late, and now he was right in his office. It was so strange and unbelievable.

"Are you serious? Then you are the man, Bogdan."

Laughing, he said, "Come on, my friend, this is Ukraine. Drinking, smoking, and sex is part of our culture. I drink every day, so it's not new."

Fred said, "I see, quite strange. I wonder how you guys cope with everyday drinking and smoking. I nearly messed up yesterday. Well, apart from that, I guess you went home with a girl last night?"

Bogdan said, "Come on, Smith, you don't know me, and moreover, Ukraine is my home. There are beautiful girls everywhere looking for someone to take them home. Before I got home yesterday, one was already waiting for me at home. I'm even tired of these girls because anytime you call on them, they will show up and seem not to be tired of the sex. How is your brother? I mean your friend Johnson?"

Fred answered, "He's good, just catching some fun with his family on Skype."

Bogdan said, "Good, say hi to him and his family."

Fred answered, "Of course I will do that for you. I called you for you need to tell me more about Natasha, how I could get in touch with her."

Bogdan said, "My friend, I thought you have forgotten about this Natasha of a girl." Bogdan's receptionist shouted, "You mean my own Natasha?" And he replied immediately "Shut up, Natasha. You're not the only Natasha in Ukraine. In fact we have about ten Natashas in this building." He continued. "So you still keep her on your mind?"

Fred said, "Yeah, she has been here on my mind, tormenting me ever since I last saw her. I can't help it any longer. Can you help me to check their websites, to know when next she's stripping, because I have no access to their websites. It requires a PIN code, and I hope you've got it because you are used to the club."

Bogdan said, "Oh! My friend, I'm sorry. I used to have access to the code, but now I don't because I'm no longer updated, and moreover, it seems their security is tighter these days. Well, I will contact a friend who may release the code for me. I will help you know her update, and I will call you back in few minutes because I've got work to do now. So should I check when next she's stripping and also when she's free for private stripping?"

Fred answered, "Yes, Bogdan, I just want to make contact with her. Thank you very much. I will be expecting your call in short time then. My regards to Natasha. I mean the one in your office."

Smiling, Bogdan said. "All right, I will extend your greetings to her."

Fred walked back to the setting room to meet James, only to discover that he had finished speaking with her family and now he was speaking with his girlfriend, Ashley. James was interrupted. "Seriously, Ashley, you didn't tell me you are still showing your booms on Skype for this dude," said Fred, and James was smiling. Ashley quickly covered her bosom, screaming at James for allowing Smith to burst into the camera. "Come on, babe, it's not fair! You didn't tell me that Smith was already here, and now he's seen my boom," Ashley shouted.

"Come on, Ashley, it's me. What is the difference between this dude and me? Just get over it," said Fred, and James, in another way, was still laughing because he really wanted Fred to see how big Ashley's breasts were.

"Come on, babe, it's all right. He's my dude. And I guess he has seen nothing much. It's just the breast," said James carelessly.

"Babe, what do you take me to be? You've gone too far this time around." She immediately ended up the call. James and Fred burst into laughter, and soon Bogdan called Fred and told him when Natasha would be free for private stripping. Fred pleaded with him to make some negotiations with BerryX because the schedule was too far and he had less than a week to stay over in Ukraine. He doubled the money for the company to shorten the more time for the private stripping, which would be in few days coming.

Inna never had legs back home last night. It was quite an absurd moment for her. It was really hard and painful, though she enjoyed it. But how could she hide these feelings from her mom? How would her mother feel? If she found out that she had sex up to the extent that she couldn't stand on her feet properly? Oh! She would be really disappointed in her because she had always been the good girl that didn't like much drinking and clubbing, but now, she was down. Inna had to do everything possible to stop her mother from knowing how she felt and what happened to her. But if she pretended she was sick, her mom would like to get her to the hospital. Thus, the only thing she could do was ignorance. She would not speak to anyone, not even her junior brother.

Karina, Inna's mother, was ready for work; she still wondered why she did not see Inna this morning, though Inna told her that she was going to spend the night with her friend Alla. Surprisingly, she came back very early this morning, and now that it was about 11:00 a.m., she was not yet out of her room. "Does it mean that she drank much last night? No, I don't think so, because Inna does not drink much. Then what is wrong with her? Why hasn't she prepared for her summer lessons?" she murmured and went straight to her door. Before knocking on the door, Karina called Eric, Inna's younger brother, to find out if he saw her this morning. "Eric!" she called, but Eric was busy with his friends downstairs, playing, but at last he answered. "Da, Mama." Yes, Mama. "You are ready for work? Hope you will come back on time to take me to the riverside in the evening because my friends will be going with their mom later today," Eric answered.

"Yes, dear, I'm ready for work and I will be back on time, but if I don't come back on time, Inna will take you to the waterside," said his mother.

"No, no, Mama, I don't want Inna to take me there. I want to go with you or with Papa. But Papa is not coming back till next week, so I want only you," he insisted.

"OK! Sweet, I will take you there myself, and you will see your friends over there and play with them too. Have you seen your sister today? I mean this morning," she asked.

"Yes, Mama, I saw her coming out from the toilet when I woke up. She seemed not to be strong. I think she might have fallen down because she walked very badly and wouldn't speak with me when I greeted her," said Eric.

"It's all right, babe, thank you. Let me check on her before I leave." Karina went to Inna's door and wanted to bang on the door, but she remembered that she had not woken her up from sleep, and if she did, she might get mad at her. But she had to wake her, so she began to knock on the door in a very soft manner and also call her name. She knocked several times, but there was no response. Then she increased her rate of knocking, and suddenly Inna shouted, "Mama, *iditieee*. Go away. Leave me alone. Why do you have to wake me? I'm no longer a kid. For god's sake, I'm not Eric."

"I'm sorry, hope you're all right. I just wanted find out if everything went well last night and why you have not left for your summer tutorials," said her mom.

"I'm OK, Mama. Please go to work and leave me alone. I don't feel like going for studies today, so just go away and don't disturb me." Karina wasn't shocked by her daughter because she knew that it must be teenage things or heartbreak because Inna behaved absurdly mostly when she had a fight with her boyfriend. Karina quietly left the door, saying, "OK, honey, just be fine, and I'm going to work."

Inna watched through the window as her mum drove out of the compound. She immediately came out from her room to clean herself up. She was in the shower for more than two hours, bathing and thinking about last night. It was really strange for her to fall so easily for this guy Fred, who gave her something different.

Inna stayed indoors for about two days before she got better and started her summer lessons again. Her mum tried to find out what really happened to her, but she kept saying that she was fine, that she needed some time for herself. Inna told her friends what happened, and they were so amazed with it. She had to leave her formal boyfriend, who was seventeen years old, because she had tasted what was more than what she was used to take, though it was her fourth time doing it. Her boyfriend, Ivan, was heartbroken, but she never gave a damn about it because right now, all she thought about was Fred, and she was ready to do anything to have him.

Inna was a pretty, sweet, clean girl that was older than her age in appearance. At first you would think that she was about twenty-two, not knowing that she just turned eighteen. Her blond hair made her extremely beautiful and amazing. She wanted something different in her life, and I guess she had got it and wouldn't let it go. It all happened that the first time she visited BerryX, the day that she met Fred and James, and now she was beginning to like Fred. She wouldn't stop talking about him. She has talked about him up to the extent that her friends were now eager to meet black guys.

Inna wouldn't stop calling Fred as the days kept passing by. She tried all her possible best to learn the English language as fast as she could so that she could communicate well with Fred, but Fred, on the other hand, had no interest in her but sex.

CHAPTER FOUR

About the Company BerryX

*B*erryX they called it. This company was located in major cities in different parts of the Russian Federation, more especially in Ukraine, where it was established. It operated heavily on entertainment and other pleasure services. BerryX had the most beautiful clubs, cafés, and hotels for relaxation and comfort. Due to its nice features and best services, it became a peaceful home for men/ladies of honor and of different calibers. It was the best home ever for leisure, business, fun, and pleasure.

BerryX pulled out more personalities compared to other clubs and cafés due to its management. It had the most beautiful girls as workers compared to other related entertainment companies, and these young girls were the major source of their capital because they created more attraction and pleasure.

At the initial stage of the company, it was quite a good company owned by an old Mafia member called Don Dmitri. Actually, the name of the company BerryX was named after his wife, Linna, who loved Berries so much. When his husband was looking for a name to call his café, she called it Berry, and her husband added the letter X in it. Don Dmitri, the mentor, started this company as a café in Kiev, the capital, and later on expanded it as a hotel/club, but it wasn't famous as other big clubs in the city. Don Dmitri had no evil thought about his company as a normal Ukrainian. He was happy with what he had, and the finance from the company was enough and satisfactory for him and his family. Though he still hoped that in some years to come, his company would be famous like the others.

A few years later, Don Dmitri fell sick due to old age and demanded that his son, Anton, who has been in military school in Moscow for the past ten years, should come back to manage the company. Anton was sent to military school by his father, Dmitri, as a result of anger. He never wanted to learn good things. He cared less about education and cared more for fun, girls, clubs, and drugs only. His father, being a big rich man, wanted the best for him, but he never cared for anything good. He never wanted to work for it. He just wanted to sit down and sleep without working. Anton came back home every night drunk, and at least once a week, he ran into one or two police problems. Either he had been caught sleeping with a teenage girl or drinking and driving, hitting someone's car, or caught with hard drugs. He was a real threat and great problem to his father and also spoiling the repute of him to the state. Dmitri had bailed his son countless times from the jail.

When Dmitri looked at all these misbehaviors by his only son, it really gave him some headaches and nightmares. He could not afford to see himself being disgraced as a result of a bad son who refused to learn. Dmitri would have given up his ghost a few months ago on heart attack due to some government problems in his office and his son's madness on raping an underage girl, which gave him a real concern. When the matter was offhand, Dmitri contacted his close friend Maxim, who was now a senior and well-ranked police officer in Moscow. Maxim suggested that he should bring him over to military school in Moscow, that he would hold him there for years until his head got better. Dmitri never failed to hasten, and he accepted the advice and sent Anton—who claimed to be in his final year in the university but had an empty head—to Moscow to start all over again in military school with no choice left. Anton felt very bad about it but had no other choice because no matter how much he would try to run, his father would still get him.

When Anton started his military school, Dmitri retired from the government work because of his age and established BerryX, as it was suggested by his wife Linna, who had been so creative and encouraging.

When Anton came back from the military academy, there were many positive changes in him, though he was now in his early thirties so he was now a man. Dmitri, at the sickbed, handed all his papers and documents of the company and also his stock properties to Anton, who never expected much from his father due to his misbehaviors. Dmitri explained everything to him, his plans and future dreams for BerryX. He also took him to some places for recognition. After a few months, Dmitri kicked the bucket, and Anton started running the company full-time.

Five years later, the company was running down instead of developing. Many branches of BerryX were closed. It was losing its customers and also workers (due to Anton's misbehaviors, sleeping with his female workers and doing all sorts of things that a boss shouldn't). Anton was so confused about it and needed to do something to still maintain the name of his father, though they were never good friends. (But he owed him one. For these responsibilities, he thought he shouldn't let him down.) Anton took a trip to Moscow to see his dearest girlfriend, Alina, that had much cared about him. Though he messed around with other bitches, she never cared. When he arrived in Moscow, he thought that Alina would be married, but to his greatest surprise, she wasn't married yet. So he quickly proposed to her because he needed a wife in his life, a wife that would assist him, and he knew that it was only Alina that would be able to tolerate and cope with him. Alina was left with no choice than to marry him because she loved him and her condition wasn't good enough for her—as in going from one club to the other every day, sleeping with different men and smoking weed. She needed a new life, so it was better for her to get married; moreover, she had aged, so she agreed to marry him, and they both came back to Kiev and wedded. It was a very big celebration, and Linna Anton's mother was very happy and proud of him for making such a good decision in his life.

Days and months passes by; Anton and Alina kept on thinking about how to revive the company, to make it what Dmitri really wanted it to be. Surprisingly for Anton, Alina spoke out her mind. The plan/suggestion was to go to typical and local villages and towns and cities to offer lots of money to beautiful girls who would love to work with their company as stewards and dancers. The way it was presented to parents, they allowed their daughters and sons to do the work; after all, life was boring in the village.

They set out the plan. Anton sent his men to different parts of the towns and nearby villages to have eyes on the beautiful girls and to offer them a contract on working with the company for a huge amount of money for a period of a year or more. The poor girls accepted the offer and began work immediately. The girls who seemed ugly / not too pretty were fired out of the company, and everything was renewed and furnished. As time went on, the company began to progress, but there were little problems with some of the local beautiful girls who were not well educated; thus, Anton had to do something about it immediately by building a private institute that he called BerryX Dance Institute. This building was located at the extreme part of the town and was very far away from other buildings. The structure of the building was classic. The building was made up of a two-story underground and a story upward. Anton spent a lot of money on building the institute and employing workers from different parts of the world on different specialties.

The girls, who signed up for a year's or two years' contract with the company, were sent to the institute to polish their languages and dance style. After the contracts, most of the girls earned lots of money and wanted to leave the company and start up their lives, but the company, knowing their values, refused to let them go but posted them to other branches of BerryX and made them to live on threats. These girls now lived on their instructions as the company gradually took their freedom by forcing them to sign life contracts. The girls now lived in fear because the company threatened to kill them and their loved ones if they ran away or disclosed their secrets to the outside world. As time went on, the company kept growing bigger and bigger. As more girls were admitted into the institute voluntarily, the rate of threats increased. It now became a black market as prostitution and drugs were involved coded. Anton started to gain lots of money from his company. His pride increased. His rate of taking drugs also increased, and he couldn't control his decisions any longer. It was then that the company went extreme. They started buying and kidnapping children from ten years and above, both boys and girls, to get better breeds for tomorrow. They had really gone extreme. More equipment was brought to the institute for different purposes. The institute is now divided into sessions and fields. The strippers, dancers, sex workers, bodyguards, bouncers, and stewards. These different sessions receive different lessons and at times the same lectures in the same hall. They live and study in the institute, and after their graduations, they are posted to different parts of the company to work. They are as perfect as they are being taught and are followed about by guards who watch over their backs.

The little girls and boys from eight to fifteen years old, who unfortunately find themselves in this institute, never find it easy, more especially the boys, who they put on diets. Some of them are castrated in order to get a bigger penises/bodies or for stronger sex. Some boys are trained in the field of being thugs/ guards. These boys, at an early age, are injected with different chemicals and foods to make their bodies bigger and stronger as giants; thus, at the age of seventeen, they are fit to go into the fields and are perfect to work. Some are trained on how to fight and kill to protect the interests of the company, but they all remain in bondage, knowing and unknowingly. The company keeps pumping them with money. They have nothing to disclose because the company bought/found some of them when they were still kids. And some of these boys were street boys that had no future, but the company gave them a future, so no regrets about it because they now live big and drive expensive cars and live in beautiful houses. But they still lacked freedom.

Also, the little girls are trained according to the company's purpose for them; some are trained in the area of prostitution, stripping, killing, and dancing. Most of the girls love what they do because they love fun. They have all been exposed to drugs and have different managers who monitor, control, and instruct them on what to do. Anyone who has ever tried to escape or disclose the secret of the company was eliminated, and moreover, BerryX has grown above the law as Anton made friends with other Mafia and politicians that kept him strong.

As years passed by, BerryX became one of the most famous clubs in the Russian Federation, Poland, Germany and so many other countries. BerryX now had its branches in famous cities. It was a club where you met the most beautiful girls as stewards, dancers, strippers, prostitutes, and entertainers. You would get whatever you wanted. "Life is all about pleasure and fun"—that was the motto of BerryX. Most of the company's buildings were well decorated and beautified like tourist centers, and this idea really attracted many customers to them because it was just unique.

CHAPTER FIVE

Private Stripping

$\mathcal{T}$ime seems not to have fled like a shooting star. It trolled like a bride and a bridegroom marching back home on their wedding day with big eagerness to arrive home to get laid. Thus, it was a day that would live never to be forgotten, a remarkable day indeed—a day that had been long waited for had finally come. Fred was so eager like never before; he felt as if it would be his first time to have a date with a girl. He was restless, thinking of how positive he wanted it to be.

"Come on, Mr. Smith, I don't think Mrs. Smith will be so eager to see you like this. Why are you acting like a high school guy who's having his first date? Get calm, she's just a stripper. I mean an ordinary stripper, not even Miss World. You can't be this in love because I have never seen you fall no matter the beauty," said James.

"Whatever, James, but I can't understand why I feel so different with this girl. I don't know why. I have tried to figure out why I've been acting like a guy on a first date, but I can't explain this feeling inside me. It's so strange and strong. It seems as if she's everything I think of and care about for now. My head echoes her voice." Fred expressed his feelings.

"I just wish I could see this Miss World that has taken your thoughts away from you, giving you nightmares and blow jobs in your dreams. Could this fact be real? Don't tell me that you're in love with a stripper like R. Kelly, because I know that very soon, you will flirt," said James.

"I'm not sure yet because I'm a little bit confused. I have never tasted real love or been in love, so I don't know what it tastes like. This feeling could be real love, but why should it take away all my guts and mantle. I have never thought about a girl for this long. Please, James, pass the Jack Daniels bottle to me. I want more drink to clear my mind."

James passed the bottle to him, smiling. "Oh! My god, I guess this trip to Ukraine will be the most interesting trip ever made. I'm happy that it wasn't Moscow but Ukraine. Fred, to be sincere, I don't know what to write about you, but it would be an interesting story to write. 'King of womanizers, falling in love with a stripper."

"Don't even try shit with me. Gosh! What am I saying, you can't write shit about love because you don't know what love is, and moreover, you have never fallen in love before. Just be sincere, will you? Or have you ever written stuff about love except crime?" Fred asked.

"Come on, dude, look at how two grown-ups like us are talking about love like two high school guys. Of course I have felt love, and I have once been in love and now am still trying to love Ashley," James spoke out is mind.

Fred laughed. "Tell me, dude, when did that happen? Where was I then? Did I travel to another planet? Dude, I have known you all my life. You're my best man, and you always tell every move you've ever taken. So you can't just tell me that you've been into real love and I didn't know, or is it Diana? The girl you had for few months when we were still in high school. Yeah, you had feelings for her. You liked her, but she broke your heart simply because you didn't look sexy and attractive to her. Truly, those days you were skinny and always shy and afraid to talk to girls, so she pushed you away and started dating Cole Walker, who had more swag and had also dated some other girls in her class. She couldn't date me because I was your friend. I can still remember the poem you wrote to her, which you practiced for months. Your brother Mike was very funny, telling you to write a poem for her on the Valentine's Day, thinking that she's going to come back to you, but she never looked back.

The Cloud

I want to live in the sky!
Where I could always see the beautiful clouds!
As it keeps rolling like a clattering diamond!
Clouds of the sky, shading rains, holding stars and the gentle moon!
A home for two souls to make love to fulfillments without distractions!
I long and linger to be in the sky that has loops and crystals for passion!
Oh, my beautiful treasure, I wish we could be in this lovely cloud and set our love on fire, a fire that is meant to be burnt forever!
There I will keep cherishing, adoring, and making you feel strong in the deepest bosom of never-ending love!

I will touch you as softly as the cloud!
We shall fly endlessly in love like a shooting star!
Then our love must shower like a rain in spring!
And this love must never go because it will be hot like
the summer sun!
It will be cool, innocent, and quiet like the dawn moon!
Clouds of the sky, shading rains, holding stars and the
gentle moon!
Let me live in the cloud close to heaven!
Then the Lord shall bless us with more love!

"Your poems never had any effect on her." Fred sighed.

"This tremor really brought you down. You wept for days, thinking that there would be no one as pretty as her again. I consoled you, brought you up, and taught you how to play around with girls. I mean the bad-guy aspect. So should I still tell you more stories?" As they were speaking, they had already grabbed their game pads, playing PS (football) and also sipping their drink.

James smiled. "You don't ever forget things, do you? I can't believe that you can still recall that very poem. High school and college life was pretty funny. So many amazing things happened, more especially when we were in high school. I remembered when you told me about your uncle Joe. Her girlfriend Jessica usually comes around by three p.m. at least four times in a week, and each time she comes, they do make love. You told me that you liked Jessica's ringing tune (the sound she makes during sex), the way she screams with lots of passion. I wanted to hear her scream also because you talked about it much. Then we aimed a target to hide under his bed at 2:30 p.m. We waited that very day, and they never showed up. It was the second time that she showed up, and without hesitation, your uncle Joe started having sex with her. Within a short time, she started screaming loud like a porn star. Her ringing tune was so seducing that we couldn't resist.

Unknown to them, we started masturbating under the bed, and when your uncle seemed to reach his climax was the same time we reached ours, and when he shouted, we foolishly shouted, forgetting that we were right under his bed. He was so surprised and disappointed in you as he chased us out from the room with great anger. Jessica was so shy, and she quickly dressed up and left your house. That was the funniest thing that has ever happened in my life. He made you miss classes for two days, and your mum punished you for that. Later on, you were angry with me because you received all the punishment alone."

Dude it was really funny. I don't know what I was thinking then. But you are the cause. You've not really heard a live ring tune, so I decided to help you experience it, but everything messed up. You know, it took Uncle Joe months to reconcile with Jessica. I couldn't believe that he would marry Jessica because their relationship seemed to be only sex, just like friends with benefits. After then, each time I visited them, they kept smiling to each other, and at last Jessica would say that 'Hope you're not going to lie under the bed again,' and we would all laugh. They are getting older, and their little boy seems to be stubborn, and he's a resemblance of me. Each time I see him, I do remember childhood days. You know, he has always wanted to fellow me to my house whenever I visit them, but his mum wouldn't allow him to follow me because I'm always too busy, and each free time I have, she guessed that I will be with a girl, which is of no doubt," Fred exaggerated.

James won against Fred again three consecutive times in the football game, which had never happened. Then Fred knew that he was emotional tormented and would overcome his nightmares, which would be over in few hours' time. He stood up and walked straight to his room without even saying a word to James. James, on the other hand, kept laughing, calling him Mr. Lover Boy that today stood his fate. That he couldn't wait to see how Natasha the stripper would get him down. James kept wondering what would happen to Fred if she messed him up, because strippers could at times be like Ukrainian weather—so unpredictable, they could change anytime.

The given time had arrived. Fred and James sat down at the bar in the strippers' paradise. They are sipping on champagne, popping mote, and being surrounded by girls who kept them company. It was really fun as there were few men in the strippers' paradise, maybe because it wasn't yet 12:00 a.m. but 9:00 p.m. the atmosphere was conducive. The strippers striped in the same manner. As the music kept on hitting, the beautiful strippers performed and stripteased endlessly with joy. The hearts of men ran out happiness instead of pumping out blood. James was so amazed with the surroundings; he felt so good for the fun he was having. Soon a steward walked to Fred and whispered in his ears to move over to the private/champagne room. She gave him the directions and also reminded him about the rules and regulations governing the strippers.

Touching of strippers was not permitted. However, some dancers and strippers were allowed to be touched during private dances if instructed. If permitted, during a lap dance, the dancer would grind against the customer's crotch while he or she (typically he) remains clothed in an attempt to arouse or bring the recipient to climax.

The game was simple; the stripper does all the stuff by herself alone. When the lights turn red or the music stops, the stripping is over.

Fred left James for the private stripping. Fred looked so smart and cute in his attire. He called attention, the way he gently walked to the stripping room. At the time he entered the room, it was pretty dark. Soon the light brightened, and he set his eyes on pretty Natasha, whose beauty had twice increased since last he saw her. Fred was short of words. He stood for a moment, admiring her great beauty and also appreciating the fact that he was standing right in front of the angel he had being dreaming about. He felt as if he was going home with her tonight. Natasha was on the mini stage, rolling on the strip pole. Soon she came down to meet Fred. She gently pushed him to the rolling chair, which stood in the middle of the golden room, making him relax. She rolled the chair again and again, dancing around him. She climbed on the little stage in the room and began her strip dance. She stripteased like never before, and Fred felt the impact. Her strip dance was so perfect and seducing that no man would be able to escape her sexual seduction as she touched every part of you. Fred was carried away as she danced back to him and ground against his crotch. Each time Fred tried to say a word to her, she closed his mouth with her finger. She kept smiling at him and stripped almost naked. She touched Fred in his amazing part and never wanted to let him go. Fred glanced at the time and discovered that he had just fifteen minutes left, and also the light in the room would soon turn red since it appeared to be mixed. He was trying to figure out how and what to tell Natasha. When Natasha reached his crotch, he grabbed her hands and drew her face very close to him as if he wanted to do something funny with her, but he just whispered to her ears, "You're so beautiful, and I like you for who you are." Natasha quickly resisted him as she pulled his hands off her body and whispered back to his ears, saying, "They are watching at us. Don't say a word. That is the rule. I'm sure the guards are already on their way to get you out of here because you've gone beyond the rule. I enjoyed stripteasing for you, so don't mess it up." (The bouncers were on their way, but their manager called them back because he knew that he was a foreigner, and moreover, they were not conversant with the language.)

"What? Who is watching at us? This is insane. What kind of management is this? Why is it called a private stripping? That is why I wanted this stripping to be at my home, but your management never agreed because I'm a foreigner," he exclaimed in a low tune. "No one should mess up with my privacy," said Fred. Natasha felt for him. She saw the feelings of her burning in his eyes. Fred spoke to her again, saying, "Why are you doing this? I mean why are you stripping? You deserve a better future than this." Natasha, who knew nothing about the future and had never been told something of this nature since a long time ago, whispered back to him, saying, "Gentleman, I love my job, and there is no future like here, so you better keep short because they can also trace our conversation as well. So if you want to watch me strip again for you, you sexy man, then better follow the rules."

Fred was now very confused and speechless as she kept winding and twisting her waist for him, in time with the music. Everything that he thought about was how he could just take her home for the night and never let her go ever again. Time was fasten, and Natasha noticed that the music would soon stop. She played it smart by rolling Fred's chair sideward, backing the microcamera. She took his pen and raised his first shirt. She wrote her number on his inner white T-shirt in a way that no one could notice. She did so because she just liked Fred and wanted to speak with him again. She immediately rolled the chair backward to its formal position, strip dancing. Fred felt released and happier for his progress, and soon, the yellow light turned red and the music stopped, indicating that time was over. In a few seconds, the light brightened again and Fred couldn't see Natasha, who was on the stage, stripping for him. He quickly left the room to join James in the strippers' paradise. Fred didn't see James around. He called and James was already in the ladies' club, having fun. Fred found his way to the ladies' paradise and met James, playing around and having fun with several sexy girls who were half-naked (they wore only pants).

"How was she, dude? I mean Natasha. Hope you had fun enough! I guess she didn't have sex with you. Come and sit in paradise with me. These girls are killing me. They are making me go high, and you know I have already had sex with one of them about twenty minutes ago in their sex room. Two hundred bucks for twenty minutes. These girls are special. There are machineries. In twenty minutes, you will feel as if you've had sex for the whole night, so go on pick any of them that you want. They are all for sex. Or I will tell them to get a menu for you where you will select the girls of your choice. Here is real." He laughed.

Fred, who looked worried, sat down, and the girls came around him and started romancing him. He got relaxed but wouldn't stop thinking about Natasha.

Fred asked one of the girls to call a steward for him. When the steward came, there was no difference between a steward and a sex worker because she also put on panties only. Even the security as well were on panties. He noticed that there was no man on service in the ladies' club. When the steward came, Fred told her that he needed a menu; she didn't understand him as she brought the menu for foods and drinks. Fred was surprised, only to find out that none among them understood any other language apart from the Russian language and the sex language. He tried to explain to her the menu that he needed, but she still never understood until she called her friend who seemed to know a little bit of English, and it also took her time to interpret what he was saying, and when she brought the sex menu, Fred finally smiled. As he browsed through the pages, the steward kept explaining the kind of girls they were—their classes, breast size, bum size, and prices as it was written. She also pointed at the ones that were present in the club for his specifications. He browsed through the pages until he got to the VIP section, and the prices he saw were like crazy (too high, twice others), and he was shocked when he saw Natasha on the list. She was the highest on the list, and the price was like boom.

"I think any man that could pay a thousand dollars for twenty-minute sex with a lady must be top class in life. How often do men pay her for sex?" Fred asked.

"I couldn't know," the steward replied. "And why do you want to know?" she asked.

"Because I'm interested in her," Fred replied.

"I'm sorry, sir. You couldn't get her even for next month because they hardly give her out for sex. She's too special as they say," she replied.

What a mess. Then why is she here on the list if she's not available?" he asked.

"I don't know, sir. Maybe you should ask the management," she answered smiling, and as she was about to leave, Fred called her attention.

"Excuse me, Marina."

The steward whore a customized chain with her name broadly written on it. "What, Mr. Handsome," she replied in the Russian language.

"Why is it that everyone in this place seems so serious? Initially you pretended as though you never heard English in your life, and at the end you spoke 50 percent of good English," Fred expressed himself.

"Sir, I barely speak English. I learned English last when I was in primary school, and I have forgotten it. I'm forced to speak because I'm left with no choice. I speak better than any other person in this place. I think my conversation with you is enough." She was about to leave, and James brought out a one hundred US dollar note and passed it to her.

"For what?" she asked.

"For being nice and sincerely speaking with me," he replied.

"Please hold your money. I do not need it, and I can't use it. I would prefer that you sleep with me," she replied smiling and left. Fred was surprise and couldn't help but keep laughing as the girls kept staring at him.

After the fun, they went back home very early (by 2:00 a.m.) because Fred wasn't comfortable and wouldn't take any girl home for the night or even pay to have sex, but James, who couldn't hold himself whenever he was a tipsy, had to take a girl back home from Fun Club.

It was 3:00 a.m., and Fred couldn't sleep due to the ringing tune produced by the girl James was with. He tried to sleep but wouldn't and could not tell James to stop having sex, so he was left with no option than to call Inna, who had been disturbing him on the phone for the past few days. When he called Inna, she was very happy to come around because she had been so hungry of him. They had a nice time, but Fred wouldn't even say a word to her but the sex, and Inna never complained.

CHAPTER SIX

Mafia Night

*I*t was about three days since they left the club. There was no sign of Natasha. Fred tried her number several times, but it never went through. It was either not available or diverted to voice mail. It gave him a lot of concern because he would be leaving the town soon, and it would be so painful and disappointing for him if he went without even saying good-bye to the girl he had ever felt for. All these thoughts kept running through his mind, and he couldn't help it. James would only laugh at him for being too calm and thoughtless because of a simple club stripper who messed him up. All he did was call on Inna to keep him company, and Inna would joyfully to come to him because she loved being around him, yet he wouldn't stop thinking about Natasha. This evening Fred was doing body exercises with James. He felt that his muscles were decreasing and for the past two days; he had not done any exercise either.

"Dude, have you confirmed our flight, or you are still hoping to see Natasha? Well, it will be good if you see her," James asked smiling.

"Please don't pretend to be nice to me. You have no feelings. All you know is sex. You won't settle down and get married. Your age is climbing like a staircase and will never come down. Why are you always afraid of responsibility?" said Fred.

"Oh! Oh! Wait, come on? What responsibility? Dude, not with a stripper that may piss me off to the street. For your information, I'm planning on settling down with Ashley before the winter, so let me enjoy my last days of being single." As they were speaking, Fred's phone rang, and James, who was closer to the phone, rushed to pick the call. He saw that it was Bogdan calling, and then he started laughing and threw the phone on Fred.

Fred answered, "Hello, Bogdan, how are you doing? Hope you're not high on this broad day." They both laughed. "Did you get my text message?"

Bogdan, sounding so Russian in his intonation, said, "Hello, my friend, I'm doing great. Everything is cool with me, and I got your text. Do you know that the Mafia are having meeting today in BerryX. I mean they are hosting the whole complex as a whole."

Fred said, "How would I know, and what does that got to do with me?"

Bogdan answered, "Come on, Natasha has something to do with you, *druq*." Laughing on the phone, he said, "If you could get into that club tonight, you can speak with her as you long as you wish because all the girls are for the Mafia tonight. There are no rules because the Mafia created the rules."

Fred seemed confused but relieved. "So how I do get to the club? I have no invitation."

Bogdan said, "That is the reason why I called you. I can help you. My friend is a friend to a young Mafia. He does business with him. He can help us get the invitation. All he needs to do is say that we are his business partners. That we have some business proposals to discuss because tonight is a business night, a night when people get opportunities to hook up with some Mafia for businesses. So it's cool, Fred."

"Wow, please do get the invitation. I will be there with James. So what's up with the payment? How will I get the money to you?"

Bogdan said, "Don't worry. You've really done enough for me. I will take care of the payment this time around. Just e-mail your names to me. I will call you when I get the ticket. Please, only suits are allowed. We will go together when it's time."

Fred said, "Bye! Catch you then."

"So what's making you so happy and amazed? I have not seen you smile for days. Is she coming to sleep with you?" asked James.

"For god's sake, be real for once. Everything is not all about sex," said Fred.

"Then what? We are here for fun. I feel like not going back if not for Ashley and my work."

"We are going to BerryX tonight. It's really going to be hot. It's the Mafia's day/meeting/conference, whatever. But we should be there," said Fred.

"I thought you said that you are not going to that club again, that your account for the trip is running down. Well, I'm ready anytime as long as I will catch my fun," James declared.

"It's not only fun, you can make a good business proposal to these guys if they are interested in international trade and some other stuff. Let's achieve something in this trip, not only the fun," Fred spoke with seriousness.

"Come on, dude, what business? I'm here for fun, not for business. Are you going for Natasha or for business?" he asked.

"I'm going for both. Come, let's stop behaving like kids and get ready for the night. Mind you, we have to be in suits."

When the time was due, Bogdan came, and they left for BerryX in the limousine cab. They were corporately dressed in suits. On arrival, they were confirmed into the conference room. They settled down in their given seats. They watched the girls as they displayed on stage, entertaining their audience with different kinds of dances. The conference room was so amazing and stylish as each party sat down in their own separate decorated table, discussing and exchanging handshakes. Soon Bogdan's friend arrived, and he introduced James and Fred to him. He loved the style of suits that Fred and James wore; they were real American outfits. Without much time, they discussed international trade, which was the most important thing to him because he was an importer. Fred and James were conversant with trade words. They never found it difficult to speak on international trade because their occupations exposed them to such business words, and moreover, the young Mafia did not understand English so strongly, so he wasn't understanding everything they were saying. Don Boris took Fred and James table to table, introducing them to his fellow business partners (Mafia). They exchanged handshakes and brief discussions with some of them that understood English. It was really fun and educative. When the conference was over, it was time for refreshments. They left the conference room for the refreshment palace that was well decorated like a paradise (they called the hall Free World). All the girls were sexily dressed and attractive. Everything was free—food, drinks, and girls. The Mafia had already taken care of the payment. Bogdan had been waiting for this day for a long time because he was going to drink the wine of his choice and have sex with a girl of his choice for free. The girls were just coming in and out and around. Men were playing with them like toys. The ladies that came with their husbands or on their own were left in the men's hall, were they would be properly taken care of by male sex workers and strippers.

"The fun had just begun for the day," Bogdan expressed himself. "So, guys, let's get acquainted as usual. Fred, could you take a look at your front? the unique golden table at your left. Can you see that man sitting over there in a white Mafia suit amidst of those men? I mean the one speaking right now and nodding his head." Fred found the target. "He is Don Anton, the mentor. He's the owner of BerryX they said. I have only seen him once. He seems to be growing younger these days," said Bogdan.

"You mean that gentleman with white beard He seems so welcoming. His business manners might have made him so prudent, so prominent, and successful in running this company. He must be a hit man for this place to be well coordinated and booming. You know, I can't remember when the last time was that I had seen club like this that has such security. The security are huge, twice me, and they are everywhere. It's safe over here. It's not easy to run a big company like this. It requires lots of discipline," Fred exclaimed.

"Yeah, Fred, you are right. Do you remember Jones Brown? Kent's father. I used to work for him in his night bar during summer holidays when we were still in high school. I know how difficult it was running just a night café. The manager kept screaming at workers, I mean the girls. It was not really easy. More fives to Don Anton, or whatever he's called," said James, and they laughed. Natasha had just finished an excellent performance on the stage with the other two girls that were as pretty as she was. Immediately after the performance, the three girls walked straight to the table where Don Anton and his friends were sitting to acknowledge them and to keep them company.

"Come over here to me, my daughter. You did great," Don Anton pledged to her, and she felt so safe and comfortable in his arms.

"Come on, Fred, those three girls over there with Don Anton are so pretty. I mean the ones that had just performed. So which among them could be Natasha?" asked James. Fred stared at the girls, and his eyes jammed with Natasha's, and they both smiled at each other. "Oh! I see, she's the one," said James, and they cheered up and toasted to Natasha. Two girls walked by. "Please, is there anything we can offer to you guys?" they asked with Russian intonations, laughing. James and Bogdan quickly grabbed them, and the girls pleasured them.

Fred wouldn't stop looking and admiring at Natasha. James was carried away already by the other girls. Natasha turned around to Fred again, and they both smiled. Soon she left Don Anton with other girls and walked straight to Fred. Fred couldn't believe it as she sat on his lap, saying "Babe boy, how are you doing? I'm sorry I have not got free time to switch on my mobile phone. This week has been a hard week, so much work. I know you might have tried to call me."

"Everything is now all right. Looking at your face alone has washed away my worries. You sitting on my lap right now is dream come true. I was thinking that I won't see you again before I'll leave town. You know, I really like your voice intonation. It's really amazing and different from others girls, and I guess I'm allowed to speak and touch you today?" Fred asked. Squeezing her in his arms.

"Oh yes, you can." She laughed. "But be careful because all eyes are always on me."

"What?" Fred asked.

"Just kidding," she replied.

"I get it," said Fred, smiling.

"So how do you want it, nice and slow or the blow jobs?" she asked.

"What?" Fred looked at her.

"Come on, handsome. I'm just pulling your leg. So tell me about you, where do you come from? I like foreigners because they do treat our ladies well with care, not like our asshole boys." Natasha smiled. "And I hope that our ladies have also treated you with care."

"Oh yes, they did. They are so sweet and simple, but you're the best," said Fred.

"Come on, I did nothing with you. I only stripped for you, so how could I be the best?" she asked.

"Natasha, you know what? I like you." As he was about to express his feelings to her, Don Anton and his entourage passed by waving.

"My young friends, hope you're having fun."

"Oh yes, we are," they replied. Natasha became uncomfortable as she wrote down an address and time for Fred where they could meet the next day for a brief lunch. "Make sure you're right there on time," she said.

"I hope you will be there because I don't like waiting," he replied.

"Clear." Natasha smiled, waving as she walked to other table and started speaking with a man who had been eyeing her.

"Jes, she's so hot. You know I'm just seeing her so close for the first time. You couldn't even introduce her to me, or are you afraid that I might sleep with her first since she is . . ." James swallowed the remaining words and continued. "No wonder your heart has been so troubled since you saw her. But I know after you have sex with her, you will still let her go. Of course she can't stay with you. She's a senior hooker," he whispered in his ears so slowly.

Fred beat him on his head. "Come on, I thought you were busy with those girls. What brought your eyes over her? I told you that I never miss a target. I will get her laid, and by the way, even if you knew, you would have given up because you don't waste time on girls as I have taught you," said Fred.

"Then what? You mean all this passion was to get her in bed? Come on, tell me what's on your mind with her, to befriend her?" James asked.

"I don't know yet. Stop pulling my leg. Where is Bogdan? He has really done great. He saved my ass."

"Oops! Your German friend should be having sex by now. He has been so busy with drinks and girls. I hope he will get better. You know what?"

"What?" said Fred.

"These girls seem too serious, as if they are in jail. I couldn't see real smiles on their faces. They just want to do the stuff and wouldn't wanna tell you any other thing. Let's forget the language thing," James complained.

"Come on, they work for the company. What do you want them to do? They follow instructions. You can't expect them to be real. Come on, dude," said Fred.

They had fun and left to a nearby artificial pool, where they spent their night.

CHAPTER SEVEN

Mystery Reviewed

$\mathcal{F}$red looked at his wristwatch over again and again and felt uncomfortable. It was in an open café. He sat outside on a windy afternoon, waiting for Natasha. She made a promise to see him today at 2:00 p.m. "It's about ten minutes late, and she's not here," he soliloquized. "This girl shouldn't piss me off the second time because I don't know what to tell James. He's going to really laugh at me and punch me in my face for postponing our flight schedule for what I'm not sure of.

"Here I am waiting for her with no hope left. Every girl around is staring at me, and some have even walked up to me, but I refused to speak with them because I'm waiting for the girl of my dreams, the one that has always been there each time I close and open my eyes. The one that my heart has been seeking for, the one that I want to stay with, the one on my mind."

Fred stared at his watch again, and it was already fifteen minutes late, and all sorts of thoughts kept running through his mind, and he felt disappointed. He was about to stand up from his seat when he heard a sound of a sports car. He looked at the direction and saw a pretty lady coming out of a red Lamborghini sports car. She was gorgeously dressed in a red dress. Every eye was on her, and when she came closer to him, he only realized that it was Natasha. She walked straight to him and gave him a peck and told him to stand up, that she did not like staying outside, that she preferred it inside.

"My lady, you look so pretty. You've got a nice car here." Fred kissed her hands, and they sat down.

"Thanks, that's one of my favorite cars." Natasha smiled. "I'm sorry for being late. I got a little delayed by my clients. Well, anyway, I'm here. So what's up with you?"

Fred breathed out. "Yeah, you are here. I was about to give up before you showed up. I thought you've forgotten and you've got no number to be called, but my mind kept telling me that you were going to show up. I would have loved us to stay outside. The weather is much cooler and more romantic out there."

He smiled. "So why do you like it inside?"

Natasha said, "Hmm, you won't understand. Some company and safety reasons. It's dangerous for me to be speaking with you without any appointment from my company. So you've got to be fast because even your cash won't be able to save your ass."

"What? I didn't get you. I thought . . ." Fred seemed confused.

"Just kidding." Natasha smiled. "So what are you eating? I have not eaten for days," asked Natasha.

"Please calm down. Don't get me confused. Don't tell me that you have spies everywhere?" Fred persisted.

"Relax, man." Natasha stared at him. "Let's forget about this and eat. It was stupid of me to tell you. Let's eat because I haven't got much time. Just tell me about yourself. I don't even remember your name. I just know that I'm coming to see one handsome chocolate, tanned boy.

"Seriously, I would take my leave now if you don't remember my name. Then why should I be dying to see you?" Fred frightened her.

"All right, Mr. Frederick, does the name matter now? Names do not matter. All that matters is that you're a friend and I want to have lunch with you. I just wanted something different this week, not all those old pals," Natasha expressed herself.

"Is that all? Hmm! You're quite interesting," said Fred, and as they were speaking, Natasha was already going through the menu and ordered for a meal without even asking Fred what he would want to eat. Fred was surprised when he saw the salesgirl bringing plates and cutlery to the table.

"So what is this that you want me to eat with you without my awareness?"

"It's called the Ukrainian bosh "*a Ukraine Soup*". I guess you've not tasted it before. I used to like this meal when I was a kid. My mama prepared this meal for us every weekend. It's been up to three months since I last ate it. I hope you will like it, just for me," she replied.

"I hope so. You're full of life and amazement. These few seconds with you make me feel different. I feel like a new person entirely," Fred admired her.

"Come on, you don't even know me. I'm not that good girl you may want to have. My history is too bad. Everything I do with men is nearly fake. I'm thought not to be real to men," said Natasha, smiling.

"Hey, I just like you, the way you are. I don't care about your work or your past. What I care about right now is the person in you that I'm seeing right now," said Fred.

"Thanks, I do appreciate your care. You do sound so kind, but I don't want you to develop any feelings for me because it's going to be a mystery. Nothing about me is real, and I like it that way." She showed Fred how to eat bosh soup, and he loved it, but not that much. "So can you now tell me about yourself," she asked.

"Hmm." Fred sighed. "I'm just like you too. Nothing about me is real but just this one thing—you are real to me. I will tell you more about me if you promise to tell me about you."

"Seriously! Oh! Why do you sound so caring to me? You hardly know me. And why should I tell you more about me when you are fake?" They both laughed.

"Come on! At least you're real to me. The feelings I have for you are real for sure. My name is Frederic Smith. You know that already. What else about me? I'm a tourist. I'm here for pleasure. I'm from the United States of America, and I live in Los Angeles. I think those are the basic things about me."

"Hmm, quite interesting, here for pleasure. It's my pleasure meeting you. I hope the pleasure and honor will be yours alone." They both laughed. "You know, today is one of my best outings. I just feel so free with you because I'm not on a mission. I don't have any negative intensions for you," Natasha expressed her feelings.

"I'm happy that you feel better. You are so amazing and sweet. Please, can you tell me about your Job? How about your future and your work? You're a beautiful lady. You deserve a better place than this present work. I see a greater personality in you. Why don't you quit that work and do something else?" said Fred.

"I love my job as much as I love myself. Look at me, I drive the most expensive current cars, I wear jewelry, I look different, like a model. I do have whatever I ever want. So many of our girls out there are dying to be like me. So I feel good doing my job, and I hope it will please you to have something so hot to do with me." She smiled with passion.

Fred felt cold and spoke out, "That smile was fake, I can tell. Because I know ladies, so please tell me, what about your parents, your friends and relatives? Are they here living in this city with you?" are they happy for you?

"What parents are you talking about? I don't have parents. BerryX is all that I have. They are my life, and I owe them," she pledged.

"I'm so sorry. What happened to your parents? Are they late?" asked Fred.

"I don't know, but it would have been better if they are late."

"Come on, babe girl, what did they do that has made you wish death on them? Look, they are your parents. Whatever they have done to you, you just have to learn how to forgive. My parents also have issues with me, but I forgave them long ago. What is it that they have done to you that is beyond forgiveness? When have you last seen them?" Fred is a tourist so he knows how to ask questions.

Natasha, feeling sober, said, "Maybe twelve or fifteen years ago. I'm not sure."

"Tell me, what happened. Why this long?" asked Fred. Natasha started to narrate a story to him.

"My life has been a tragedy. I don't know where to begin. It all happened like a dream. It was so fast. I could barely remember it all. I woke up one morning and saw myself in a big compound with lots of beautiful young girls like me, and in a short while, I only discovered that there was no way out and nowhere to run. Though life in there was quite better."

"I don't get you. Life where?" Fred seemed confused.

Natasha continued. "When I woke up from that longest tragic sleep of my life, my eyes were so blurred, and I doubted my thoughts if it was present reality. All my thoughts were that I'm in a hospital. 'But how did I manage?' I asked myself. Soon it became clear when an old male doctor walked up to me to find out if I was awakened. He tried to make me talk, but I was too weak to lift up my lips because my little self was full of confusion. Soon he called a lady that requested for my presence. The old doctor in his big eyeglasses and long beard asked me to get up. I quietly and slowly got up. He walked me up slowly through a narrow, long passage to her. I could hardly see, and my head kept echoing. I was so weak and tired. I felt like sleeping more. 'Hey, little head! Are you still feeling sleepy? You have been sleeping for two days now,' she expressed herself, and my eyes became a little bit cleared.' I'm Alyona, your primary trainer. You will take orders from me and no one else. This is now your new home. What is your name?' Alyona asked. Alyona is a woman in her late thirties. She looks very serious and scary. I could only hear her voice echoing in my head and tried to figure out what she was saying, but I couldn't speak out no matter how hard I tried. She looked at me all over again and wondered why I couldn't even say a word. After a few moments, she called on another specialist, who seemed unfriendly as he carried me on a wheelchair to his laboratory to examine me again. I had no strength to speak, to tell him that I'm all right. He injected me, and after a few minutes, he placed two bags of drip on me.

"A day later, I was able to speak, and then I realized that I wasn't in the hospital."

"Then where were you?" asked Fred.

"I couldn't know by then. All I could see around me were beautiful things. Beautiful young girls like me. I was taken to a room. It was like a dorm entry, and there were ten other girls in the room. They were exactly my age-mates. Alyona told me that they were my sisters. I tried speaking with them that very night, but no one could speak up, and I have always been that shy girl, so I quietly lay on my bed and slept off. The following day, we started lectures on language courses, and a timetable was given to us. So it is an institute? I asked myself. But it wasn't because the following day, Alyona told us that we were special, and there were also other special people like us in different departments in this building, that we will be trained for dancing and entertainment. That was how they started teaching us different kinds of dance techniques on how to entertain the audience. We learned very fast because we were forced to. Eighteen hours of the day we used for training and learning different things. We had limited time for fun. We were exposed to different kinds of drugs and medical applications. We were even placed on a diet. We had less sleep but more exercises.

"Life in there was pretty cute and better for me because there was no one to make jests and laugh at my dirty and smelly dresses, which I wore to classes most times when my papa refused to buy soap and used the money for drink. I missed nobody but my drunken father, Andrei, who cared less about me, and my Mom,

Sasha, who left us when I was seven. So I don't think that I will ever be free and normal again, and the life BerryX has given has really made much impact on me. They have taken charge and control of my life. I can hardly do anything on my own without being controlled." She wept and regretted ever reflecting back. Fred held her hands and pulled her toward his arms, consoling her. She repelled him, trying to console herself, pretending as if she was fine.

Fred said, "Babe girl, you might have gone through hell. I could see the pains of the past in your eyes. I'm so sorry for letting you remember the hard times, but I want you to listen to me. The happiness and freedom you've been seeking for, I will definitely give them to you. It's a promise. I will make sure that I get you out of this bondage. You will live a normal life again." Natasha, who seemed to have returned to her senses, quickly glanced at her wristwatch and remembered who she was. She quickly looked around and told Fred that she would be going. Fred was so surprised.

"Calm down, babe. What's the matter? Please stay with me for a while. I thought you said that you are free today," asked Fred.

"You don't even know a bit about the people I work for. They follow me everywhere I go. They will eliminate anybody who stands in my way. I'm here alone because today is my free day. If not they would have been outside somewhere around, spying at me. I have spent enough time with you. I don't want to risk you or put you on a problem. I don't want them to start monitoring my movement on my free days, please!" she begged.

"Natasha, please do feel safe with me. No one can hurt me for you. The way I feel for you, I have never felt for any other girl in this world, and I know it's love that I have seen in you. If truly it's love, I will fight to make you right. Please stay a little while with me. I can't close my eyes without seeing you."

Natasha felt very weak because no one had told her such sweet words since a long time ago. "Please, Fred, don't tell me about love. I don't want to hear about it. It's against my rules. What I need from you is to pleasure you. I want to have fun with a sweet chocolate guy like you, not for money but for fun, not for the company but for fun, and not to fall in love with you because love stings.

"BerryX took the most amazing thing in my life from me, and I won't ever forget about it, and also I won't let you fall in love with me because all who ever tried got themselves killed.

"What do you mean killed?" asked Fred.

Natasha began to narrate a story to him about her first love Vladimir.

"Vladimir was his name. The guy I have ever first loved in my whole life. He was so strong, sweet, soft, and innocent. But they took him away from me.

"How?" Fred asked.

She continued.

"From traces of the past, I and Vladimir were brought into the institute almost at the same time, but I never knew him until my final year in the institute. We started having lectures in the same class and doing most things in common because we were both trained for a similar job. Every evening, he usually came to the ladies room to make fun of us because he was allowed to do whatever he wished due to his humbleness and devotion toward his career. He was proud of himself for the work he would be doing for the company because he never had good plans for the future before the company picked him up from his village.

"Vladimir was the guy who took away my virginity and fell in love with me after he was instructed to have sex with me for his duty's perfection and fulfillment. He was the best guy in the institute, and all his desires were given to him by the directorate because he was considered as the best guy. He was the most handsome guy in the institute, and his work in the company was to make love with the VIP ladies who requested for it. He was sex skilled and also romantic. He was a king in lovemaking, even without sex, and he could make a woman reach her climax in five minutes. He was the kind of guy that every woman would like to lay hands on. His blue eyes attracted every woman to him. I was also trained, also as a VIP stripper, and due to my beauty, I was considered to the best girl and was also treated in a different way, like a princess. My virginity was considered to be important to the company in my first four months of stripping, depending on my rating by men. In my second month of stripping, men started to apply for sex, and the company kept increasing my rate/value because they knew that I was not ready yet, and moreover, I have not had sex before. I was so young but looked more mature due to the training that I had undergone. I was fourteen years old when I started my stripping career. I used to be a very shy girl, but everything changed as I became a strong, smart, pretty angel. When Vladimir graduated from his training, they offered me to him to make love, and he was so glad and happy making love the first time with the most beautiful girl he had ever seen, as he expressed himself. All my educators/doctors gathered and watched us through the camera as we made love. They watched how he made love to me. His techniques were so perfect. I kept on screaming, and there were tears all over my face while Vladimir was so happy after the sex. As days kept growing, Vladimir fell in love with me, and we both began to like each other, and the company, who knew what they were doing, gave us some privacy as we loved ourselves and had sex again, and it was against the rule. We both worked in the same café, and after the club, they would allow Vladimir to drive me back home or to the institute because I was still on practice. At the cost of driving me back home, he would drive to a lonely place where we had countless sex in the car, but these feelings never stopped us from being active from our various jobs.

Soon I discovered that I was pregnant after two months of being with Vladimir. The company, instead of being mad with me, was calm and started nursing me and posted Vladimir to a different city, Donetsk, so that he won't be emotionally disturbed, though he had failed because he was thought never to feel and to fall in love and he failed, and the company also pardoned him because it was the company's plan that we should both get together so that I will give birth to a beautiful prince or princess who will work with them and make more money for the company in future. But I and Vladimir never knew that it was the plan of the company for us to come together. When Vladimir was transferred to Donetsk, I felt very bad and helpless, but my teachers made me strong again. Vladimir could only come and see me once in a while. He was also threatened to forget about me, and he did for a while.

"Seven months later, I gave birth to a princess at the age of fifteen. I started my stripping work again about five months after childbirth. The company took the responsibility of taking care of the babe. After a few years, the babe grew bigger, and each time Vladimir saw his daughter, he felt so bad because he knew what the company was going to do with her tomorrow. As time went on, he began to fight for the little babe and my freedom, and at the cost of making issues, he was slowly eliminated, killed. When the news got to me that Vladimir was dead in a car accident, I cried and cried because I told him not to fight back, that he couldn't beat them all, but he never listened to me, and now he's dead. How can he get his daughter's freedom? I wept, and after few months, I forgot about him and life went on. I have never told anyone this story before because I don't want to remember the past and I don't want the past to spoil my present happiness."

"It's a sad story. So your daughter is with the company. This is insane. How wicked could this company be? What kind of government is this?" Fred wept I will get you both out of this bondage. I promise, I will do whatever I can to put this company down for you."

Natasha laughed. "Please don't disturb yourself. BerryX is well connected, and Anton seems to be above the law." Natasha stood up, and they both walked to her car.

"So when am I going to see you again? And where would I start with this company?" Fred asked.

"Don't worry, you will see me again. I will pay you a visit in my free time. Give me your address. I want you to remember me when you're gone," said Natasha.

"But, babe, I'm going nowhere without getting you out of this shit." He brought out the address of his apartment and gave it to her.

She smiled. "Quite near. Come on, get into the car. Let me give you a ride, it's my direction."

Fred smiled back, saying, "In that case, give me your keys, and let me show you the fun of this car." Without hesitation, she gave him the key, and he drove off.

"You're really good in driving. How do you drive this car so perfectly like someone who has been riding it for years?" she asked.

"I used to have a black Lamborghini before I gambled it out," he answered.

"I thought as much." They both laughed.

CHAPTER EIGHT

Suspect

$\mathcal{T}$he time was five in the morning. Natasha was so exhausted for the day. She stripped all night and had to go home for rest. Her second manager, Alisa, whom she had being working with for several years, called her when she was about to drive off home. Natasha was so surprised when she saw the incoming call because she had been with her all night and she never complained or called her attention. So why was she calling her now that she was exhausted? Natasha refused to answer the call because she was so tired and afraid to return to the club, but Alisa called back again, and Natasha had no choice but to answer the call. When she answered, Alisa only told Natasha to see her in her office as soon as she was awake for the day, that they had an important discussion. Natasha was confused as she drove off; she wondered what the matter could be.

Natasha overslept because of tiredness. When she woke up, it was about 1:00 p.m. She felt like sleeping again, but she remembered that she had an appointment with Alisa. She quickly dressed up and called Fred on the secure line, which he gave to her. She called him just to tell him how much she missed being around him and also thanking him for the fun and new life of happiness that he has given to her. She ended the call by telling him that he was the best friend that she has ever had for giving her hope and reason to live. After making the call, she kept the phone at home and drove off to Alisa's office, who demanded for her presence. Getting to Alisa's office, Alisa was just strolling around her office, seeming worried and gesturing around, and when she saw Natasha, she breathed out heavily; she sighed.

"Oh!" Alisa spoke in Russian. "You are here. I was so worried thinking that you won't come on time. I was about to leave my office to go to the institute. Well, it's good that you are now here."

"What is it all about? Do I need to follow you to the institute? I hope all is well!" Natasha questioned.

"No, of course, I have asked for your presence because I wanted to ask you some few questions, and I want you to be sincere with your answers," said Alisa.

"All right, I'm listening," Natasha replied.

Alisa walked close to Natasha's seat and looked into her eyes with passion and spoke out. "What is happening to you? Are you lost with confusion? Have you forgotten who you are?" Natasha seemed confused and tried to loop back to see where she had gone wrong but couldn't reflect immediately. Alisa continued. "The smiles and happiness I saw on your face last night seemed real. I observed it a few days ago and thought it was just nothing, but your outlook last night and endeavors really convinced me that there was something behind it. So tell me, what is it all about?"

Natasha wondered about with focus. "I don't know where you are driving to, but I know that I'm fine, but what's the matter with my smiles?" she confidently asked.

"Don't swallow the guilt to tell me that everything is fine with you. I have been your guardian for the past five years. I know when things go wrong with you, and it's my duty to confront you to correct your weakness. Despite the fact that you are the number one girl in this company, it does not give you the right to do what you wish. You are still under my supervision, and that is more reason why you have to start talking to me," said Alisa.

Natasha was not too good in argument and conflict. She never knew what to say because she was used to Alisa's query at least twice every month. It all started when Don Anton started using her for delivery (to pass a message to the top men in the state or to deliver drugs) instead of Alisa, who was in the best position to be a deliverer because she was worth it (she has worked for several years for Anton). Anton's reason for using Natasha was that she was beautiful and would entice men for a quick response. After this incident, Natasha got her partial freedom. (She no longer lived in the institute or their lounge in BerryX. She was given a separate apartment, but with lots of security monitoring her.) But Alisa felt that Natasha had taken her place, though she was under her control and she was looking forward to see her fall. She didn't care about her importance to the company. Natasha, on the other hand, never disobeyed or did things that would make her angry because she knew her intentions, and would do everything possible to avoid problems and maintain peace. Ever since Natasha started to live alone and deliver, her threats had really increased. She thought that it would be better outside than the walls of BerryX to free her enemies, "her fellow girls that are jealous of her in the institute." But all that wasn't real. Even the outside world was more dangerous because of what she did, "being more exposed to more drugs." Sometimes, the men she delivered to would force her to take a lot of it, and she would be left with no choice.

"Please, Alisa, tell me where I have gone wrong so that I can make it right. I have some deliveries to make."

"Hmm! I see, you have some deliveries to make. You are going nowhere until I'm sure that you're clean. And I hope Alexander will be pleased to know that you are hiding something from me," said Alisa. Alexander was Natasha's manager.

"Why are you making things difficult?" Natasha was trying her possible best not to bring out her other part, anger, in order not to make things harder. Since Natasha became more exposed to drugs—cocaine—she was careful in whatever she did because the last time she grew angry, she behaved like a mad woman, beating up Darya, a team leader of the girls who hates her in the institute, up to the extent of death, with Natasha ending up in the institute's medical center, where she stayed for a week before they released her. And she knew what passed through the medical sector and didn't want to end up there again, so she learned how to control her feelings.

"Look, all I want from you is for you to tell me that which you are hiding from me or afraid to say, but I see that you're not ready, so I will make it clear to you now. Natasha"—she called her name—"tell me, are you having affair with our business client? Of course, there are so many clients, but I mean Smith."

Natasha became weak and had to tell the truth. "Yes, I have been seeing him. He is just my friend. I love being around him because he's funny and nothing else, and by the way, he will be leaving the town soon."

"Oh! I see, just friends. Hope you have not forgotten who you are. When do you start taking laws into your hands and disobeying the rules? You have to be careful and watch your back. Just try to fix this mistake. I have my eyes on you as usual, so I advise you to be watchful before you regret your decisions," said Alisa.

Natasha was very weak as she walked out from the office. Alisa never wanted to take any chances because two years ago, she lost a girl that was under her supervision. Her name was Katir. Katir was one of the top girls in BerryX. She fell in love with a client and wanted to expose the company to him by planning to marry him before the company took her unaware and had to kill them both. Anton was very mad at the incident because Alisa did not tell him on time. Now Alisa had to call Alexander to tell him what she had noticed about Natasha so that he would alert Anton, who would be proud of her.

Alexander wasn't surprised when Alisa told him about Natasha because his boys had already briefed him about the situation and told him that Fred wasn't a threat to the company because he was just here for luxury, and moreover, he would be living soon. But notwithstanding, he had to tell Anton and brief him about the situation. As he was about to call Anton, Natasha called him.

Natasha said, "Hello, I have the package. Whom will I deliver it to?"

Alexander said, "Your voice sounds strange. Hope all is well with you?"

Natasha said, "Yeah! I think."

Alexander said, "All right, the code for the package is 23912. Be careful. He's an addict. He may delay you, but if anything goes wrong, don't hesitate to call."

Natasha said, "All right, I will be on my way in an hour to his basement."

Alexander said, "The road will be clear for you. Report to me as soon as the job is done. You will not be working tonight. You need to take a nap. Meet me at the strippers' paradise tonight. We may also have a talk."

Alexander ended the call and called Anton immediately to brief him on matters at hand and the company's progress. (Alexander was one of the top-ranked managers in BerryX. He made most of the decisions.)

Anton was at home, playing with his son, when Alexander called him. He was quit disappointed in him because Alisa had already called him concerning Natasha, but Alexander told him that Natasha was not the matter at hand, that there was so much other work to be done, not Natasha. He also told him that he was taking care of Natasha's issue and he was very disappointed in Alisa, who just called him a minute ago concerning Natasha, and now he had also called Don Anton to inform him, which was his duty, which meant that she couldn't handle matters by herself, Alexander expressed himself. Anton only asked him to be careful with such issues because he couldn't afford to lose Natasha; she had really contributed a lot to the company's progress.

Anton had never liked black men as much, more especially the ones from America. He was always afraid of them because they were always ahead in plan and wanted to find out everything. It reminded him about his old life in the police academy—how his black supervisor, Edward, punished him every day until he learned a particular skill that he wanted him to acquire/learn.

CHAPTER NINE

Anton's Life in Military School

*W*hat a punishment, what banishment, what a suffering and pain to lazy Anton. Imagine, how could a lazy Anton survive in military school? The challenge was so difficult and indisputable. At first, his father never told him that it was a military school; he only told him that he had found a good new institute in Moscow for him and he would be leaving for Moscow the following week, that he should get ready. Anton tried to say no, but his mother persuaded him that he should go, that he would be coming home every weekend or anytime he felt like. Then he agreed due to the fact that he loved Moscow and there was more life and fun in Moscow, even more than there in Ukraine (Kiev). The following week, Anton's parents saw him off to the airport, and he flew to Moscow. Anton was so pissed off in the airplane because he didn't drink a lot as expected.

Arriving at Moscow, Anton was very happy because he felt that there would be more fun and drinks and there would be no parents to stop him. To his surprise, his father's friend Maxim, who was a major police officer in Moscow, came to the airport himself to pick him up. This wasn't good at all for Anton because he hated these policeman Maxim. He had seen him twice, and the first time was when he was about six years old. Maxim visited his father because his father had an operation that nearly got him killed. Maxim stayed about a week with them. He was so scary to Anton, and Anton never liked him because he didn't allow him to play as he wished or do what he wanted. The second time was when Anton was already fifteen years old and Maxim came to Kiev for some security issues with the Ukrainian government and decided to spend some nights with them, and throughout his stay, Anton was never seen outside due to the fact that Maxim threatened him as a policeman that if he left the house without good reasons, he would make sure that he would never walk with his legs ever again. Maxim threatened him because Dmitri had briefed him about Anton's behavior, and he wasn't happy about it. When Maxim went back to Moscow, Anton was very happy, and that very night, he flew to a nearby club with his father's new Range Rover to have fun that he didn't have for the past three days. In the club, he drank and smoked a lot and was drunk driving back home and had a fatal accident that nearly took away his life. It was a pity; he stayed in the hospital for months before he could recover fully. Dmitri and Linna where speechless and confused. It was after the accident that they began to have at least a little time that they never had for him, and it was pretty late. Right from the time when Anton was three years old, his parents never had a lot of time for him due to their working status. Dmitri was a high-class government worker, and so was Linna. They devoted all their time to the government and had limited time for fun and for the family, but they were happy with their jobs because it was fetching them lots of money, making their standard of living adequate, and they could purchase whatever need they wanted. Due to less time for the family, they had someone that took care of Anton after school, and most of the time, their driver brought Anton to Linna's office. There he would stay until she finished her work for the day. There was limited time for Anton, though he was giving his best and had his own car and special driver at the age of ten. So Anton grew up basically without much time and love from his parent. This very reason made him have less respect for them. Whenever they tried to correct him, he told them that they never had time for him so they should leave him alone, and they were left with no choice. Anton only respected his late grandfather, who taught him how to be strong. Linna had to retire and start up another work so that she could at least have time for Anton after his accident, but there were no changes. But Dmitri never had time. He kept on telling Anton that a boy who wanted to be responsible would always be no matter the circumstances around him. So why had Anton decided to be lazy about life? What else did he wants from him? To leave his work and sit at home with him? "Never, I can never do that," he expressed himself.

Anton was so angry and surprised when the airport security man took him to a black van, and when he entered, he saw Maxim and greeted him so weakly, as if the world was coming to an end. But Maxim, who didn't use to laugh, smiled at him for the first time, saying, "You are welcome, son. Just feel free with me. No difference between me and your father. We are one. I grew up together with him as his best friend, so from now on, I will be your father for a while. I just want you to be a good son." He smiled again, but Anton never smiled back because he knew that it would not be fun for a man like him to be caged and not be able to make his own decisions.

"You see," Maxim continued speaking, "my dear, your father is very lucky to have a son. I have ever wished to have my own son, but I have only daughters." Anton smiled. "And they are married." Anton became sad again. "I wanted to have a son who will be like me, a son beside me that I can drink some vodka and make some jokes with." As he was speaking, Anton was already thinking about what he was going to miss at home and how his freedom would be tied in Moscow. A second thought came to him. He would definitely run away back to Ukraine or another city in Russia if the conditions became harder for him to accumulate. He also reflected back, hating himself for not drinking much in the airplane simply because of the pretty girl, Alla, sitting beside him in the first-class cabin. She told him that she did not like guys who drank much, so due to the fact that he was already admiring her, he limited his drinking. So if not, he would have been drunk by now and wouldn't be able to listen to what Maxim was saying to him.

Surprisingly to him, Maxim pressed a button and brought out whisky. He served for both of them as he toasted with him, saying, "Welcome to Moscow, my son." Anton partially smiled and was a little bit relieved as they drank in the van, laughing like best of friends, which he had never done with his father. Soon, they arrived at Maxim's house. It was like the mayor's house. It is a very big compound, well decorated like a paradise, and surrounded by security men. Anton was very surprised and never expected Maxim to be so rich. He was well welcomed, and he immediately took a shower and came over to the dinner table to join Maxim and his family for dinner. What a sweet home made up of three beautiful daughters and a wonderful wife Anton admired, and they started eating, jesting like one family. They all showed Anton love, and he began to relax. There were drinks of any kind in the sitting room, and he was allowed to drink as he wished. Marinna, Maxim's wife, liked Anton and took him like his own son, which they never had. They smoked and drank together always because she liked fun so much; even at her old age, she looked pretty and sexy. Anton was enjoying the company and was also forgetting club life because he drank at home and girls came around and he slept with them, so he was satisfied at home. It was a surprise to him for he never expected Maxim's home to be as this sweet. His first week there in Moscow was one of his best weeks in his life, and he wished never to go back again to Ukraine.

The following week, Maxim called him to the sitting room to drink. As they were drinking, he was giving him some nice advice and also reminded him why he had come to Moscow. That he would be leaving for the institute in two days' time, so he should have fun as much as he could, because in the institute, there would no fun (but Anton never understood what he meant by "there would be no fun"). A day to the day, he would be leaving for the institute, which he never cared to ask about. He went out with Lisa, Maxim's last daughter, who married a pilot a year ago, and he traveled for a national assignment, so Lisa was hanging out with her mum at home. So this night, after much jesting and drinking with Anton, whom she called brother, she decided take him to her favorite club in Moscow. As they were about to leave, the security men at home wanted to follow them because Maxim instructed them that wherever Anton was going, they should be monitoring him or go along with him so that he wouldn't look for drugs. Anton persuaded the security man to let them go alone because he would be leaving for the institute the following day, that he wanted to have fun, and they let him go. They drank more in the club and had lots of fun but couldn't control themselves as they started kissing each other and later had sex in the car that night before going home.

The next day, Lisa couldn't look at Anton's face because she was married and had sex with him, though she enjoyed it. They all waved him good-bye as Maxim accompanied him to the institute. At arrival, to his greatest surprise, it was a Military academy. Anton was weak and very angry when Maxim left him at the first gate of the academy with just the words "Son, here is now your new home. You will grow up here to become a real man. I will come asking after you as time goes on and will make sure that you are provided with anything you wish." He waved Anton off. Anton was confused and speechless to see him going. Maxim's guards led him to his executive van. Anton was taken into the academy by some huge policemen, who commanded him to follow them, and they led him to his cabinet and gave him his required items. The police academy was just like a prison; it was located some distance away from residential houses, and no cell phones were allowed into the academy.

Anton was left hopelessly with no decision than to adjust to the environment. He had no phone diaries and had no phone number in his head at least to call his parents to tell them about his situation. The training was so difficult for him, but learned to endure and accommodate. He was the most lost person in the academy. He wasn't strong, but they forced him to be. He had lots of enemies because he grew wild and wouldn't let anyone to make a decision for him. Days and years passed; he was just growing wild and wiser. He made so many friends, more especially his teachers and security men, to whom he gave money to get him drugs and to allow women to come into his cabin. He had a lot of money with him. Maxim kept sending money to him and making things OK for him, and he kept getting wiser and stronger. After four years, he decided to speak with his father and mother on phone. He spoke so maturely like a man who had so many responsibilities, and Dmitri was really impressed and thankful to Maxim. His mother was very happy speaking with him because she tried as much as she could to get in touch with him, but there was no way. She cried for days, thinking that her son would never come back to her again.

Anton gained a lot of military ranks in the academy, and his friends where posted to different police departments in the Russian Federation, but he still wondered when he would be through with the academy, and moreover, he had a lot of satisfaction. Instead they retained him as a worker in the police academy.

CHAPTER TEN

The Fight

$\mathcal{T}$ruthful words can be very hard to say when there is a problem or probation. But the fact remains: the truth shall set you free no matter how difficult the judgment may seem to be. The act of you being right will definitely prove you innocent when the dawn comes.

Alexander had begun to lose trust in Alisa because she took laws into her hands and had underestimated him by calling Anton concerning Natasha's issue. Notwithstanding, Alexander was able to predict what Alisa was about to do by taking laws into her hands because she wanted herself to be force promoted without knowing the fact that nothing would hurt Anton like losing Natasha, who had really contributed a lot to the growth of the company.

It was a Good Friday evening. The club had started, and everything seemed normal and perfect. Alisa was still looking around in search of Natasha. She couldn't call her on cell phone because it was not part of the company's routine to remind workers that which is right. Alisa wondered why she was not around. The fact that she was not stripping for the night did not give her a warranty to stay at home. She needed to be around in case there was urgent requirement for her presence by the management. Alisa had already started suspecting her being with Fred, the black American. She left her office and proceeded to Alexander's office to pull his leg.

When Alisa stepped into Alexander's office, the two naked girls playing with him immediately gave him some privacy.

"You are not supposed to be here. You should be on your duty, taking care of the girls," said Alexander. Alisa pretended as if she didn't get what he said and stretched her hands toward his body, trying to romance, him but he resisted.

"I know that I should be in my basement, but nevertheless, I have come to you instead of calling on the phone as usual, but it's a serious issue concerning your management, and I needed a face-to-face discussion."

"Hmm! My management. Why don't you go to Anton to lay your complains concerning my management as you did earlier? Come on, Alisa, what is the problem with you? Have you forgotten that I am in charge here?" asked Alexander. "I will advise you to stop shouting because it won't help matters. You've forgotten that you also have hidden issues here that I'm aware of, so don't make me remind you of the past. Things get confused at times that no one would be able to give a clear explanation. I wouldn't want to take any chances again because if I should lose any of my girls again, the blame will be on me, that I'm a bad guardian, which may end up my life. So can you please tell me where Natasha is right now? She's supposed to be here like every other girl even though she's your delivery girl. She's not the only girl that delivers. Why don't you leave Natasha alone? She's getting weird because the workload is too much on her. Can you afford to do what she does?" he asked.

"Hmm, I see the workload is too much on her, but how would I tell you that the work load has become heavy on her, because right now, as we speak, she's with Fred, massaging his back. Don't tell me that you're not aware of what is happening? Or you are pretending not to!" said Alisa.

"I'm still looking into the matter, but I guess she's at home and not with any client. She should be on her way here because I have asked for her presence," replied Alexander.

"I see, but what If I tell you that the security has confirmed that she's there or was there today?" Alisa asked.

Alexander seemed worried and confused. "Then that will be my problem to take care of. So you can go back to your duty and stop bothering me." Alexander sounded so worried because he liked Natasha and wouldn't want anything bad to happen to her. Natasha had been so decent and honest in her work, and moreover, he had feelings for her a long time ago, which she repelled.

Alisa left the room, saying, "I hope it won't be a pain in your neck because I have already sensed it, and I will be pleased to be of help."

Alisa left for the girls' dressing room, where she enlightened the girls on what to do and places to be at the rightful time. It wasn't quite long when Natasha arrived seeming strong and pretty happy. She walked straight to Alexander's management base, but he wasn't there. She strolled to his main office, where he shouldn't be at the present time, and met his angered situation.

When Alexander saw the smile on Natasha's face, he became calm but still troubled in his spirit. Natasha walked to him and gave him a pretty kiss, smiling and saying, "I didn't expect you here. I have not seen you like this before! Where are the girls that should be around you?"

Alexander said, "When will you start caring about me? Hmm." He sighed. "I see! Alisa might be right. So tell me, Natasha, why are you not here on time as usual, and moreover, I personally wanted to see you, Natasha."

Natasha, who seemed to be high, kept smiling as if everything was all right. "Alex! You know that I had a hit with the man I delivered to. I was forced to take a lot of it just for a test. You already know about it, so I am very tired, and moreover, you know that I have issues with Alisa, so please keep me out of it. I'm beginning to lose control over my senses ever since you brought me out from the walls of BerryX."

"I would believe every word that you say as usual, but I can't help the situations now. The pressure is getting high, and I'm afraid you might go for probation until your so-called friend Fred is gone from this country before he causes havoc," said Alexander.

Natasha's eyes got cleared. "What are you talking about? What probation?"

"I couldn't believe the security cameras that I have just received from the security management. I've asked them to send me the videos about you for the last five days so that I will know where to begin with you and your feelings before Alisa goes further than me. What were you thinking? Kissing your clients, it's improper, it's not allowed, but why should you of all people go against the rules? Yes, the camera got you two days ago. He was even the one that drove you home after your performance, and you kissed him in the car, which implies that you slept in his house that morning.

You would have been sent back to the institute on probation right away if Alisa had set her hands on this very video. So tell me, what has come over you?" he asked.

Natasha seemed hapless and guilty for her recent activities with Fred. she walked through confusion and tears flowing from her eyes. I'm so sorry. I just liked him as friends and nothing else." She apologized.

I would have sent the guards to go and get him for tampering with your emotions, which might as well result to his death by now. God save him that he's from the United states. But that won't stop us from getting him. I want you to go and fix this mistake of yours. Tell him to go far away from you, and if I see him near you ever again, you know what I will do. Hence forth, the security will start being with you everywhere you go." Alexander spoke out his mind.

Natasha walked out from his office in pain and drove back home. She couldn't sleep. She kept thinking and crying. It was then that she only realized that she had developed feelings for Fred, which would be the beginning of the end of her life. She had to put a stop to it before something bad happens. Also by tomorrow morning, the guards would start following her about around the city—that is, even if she didn't go to probation. Natasha stood up, took some drugs, and drove off to Fred's apartment. On her way to his apartment, she drove so rough on the lonely street without even minding the traffic lights. The police chased her and stopped her. When the police saw her, they became speechless because she was sexily dressed as usual. One of the cops insisted that she should show vehicle papers and her driving license. She looked for it but couldn't see it due to being high and angry. The cop asked her to come down from the vehicle for searching. She was confused and also speechless; it was then that she remembered who she was by calling her company concerning the police harassment. Within a few minutes, the police apologized and let her go.

When she arrived at Fred's apartment, James and Fred were busy still mapping out their plans and attack to BerryX. Natasha seemed wild and unusual. Fred ran to her.

"Sweet babe, what is the problem? You look so different," said Fred.

"Please don't touch me again. I warned you but you wouldn't listen. You can't fight them, and you can't force me to be normal ever again. Look at me," she wept. "Please, I don't want to see you near me anymore. It's no longer safe with you."

"Be calm, babe. Whatever they have said to you is not true. We can beat them. Don't be weak. You can't ask me to stop when I'm already done. Look around this room. The walls of the room are filled with maps, both interior and exterior directions of BerryX and the institute, which you've helped us with. We shall be attacking them soon. I'm waiting for the rightful time, and you will be freed. You will live a normal life again, even without me if it's your wish," said Fred.

Natasha shouted, "I don't want to live a normal life again. I love the life I lived before. Now my thoughts are filled with confusion. All I want is that you leave me alone. Here is your phone." She threw the secured line on the table. "Don't bother coming to me ever again for they will hunt you down. I don't want anyone to die any longer because of me." She moved toward the wall and began to tear off the maps. Fred was tired of her because the more he tried stopping her, the more she resisted, and James on the other side got annoyed and walked out of the room, for Natasha destroyed what had taken several days to build.

Natasha made up her mind. Fred tried stopping her, but she refused him and walked away fast, crying. She entered her car and was about to drive off. Fred kept on pleading, but she never listened as she drove off with lots of tears on her face.

Fred walked into the sitting room with lots of anger on how to make sure that BerryX got destroyed before he left the city.

"What a mess, I'm so pissed off and disappointed. Can't you see that you can't damn change her life? Let's gets out of this country for there's no justice. Look at what she has done to you, tearing you apart with emotions. She isn't worth it. I'm leaving this country today. I can't stand this any longer. You've being keeping here for the past weeks, and every work that we've done because of her has been just destroyed by her." James grew angry.

"James, don't say that. Can't you see that she's insane and confused? They have found out about us and have threatened to kill her. We must stop them now. I need to call Bogdan and the other guys because tonight BerryX is going to know that they have gone too far," said Fred.

"Hmm! What are you talking about? That is murder. You want to strike when the maps are all gone. It's a bad idea. This guy's got a lot of well-trained security. Striking now is not an option because you may never see her ever again. Let's keep to our early plan," said James.

"James, I still have all the maps on my phone. I will call Leila to help me hack into their navigation system again and then send live cameras to me, for I have got to shake them a little bit tonight to see the reaction," said Fred.

"Bro, you better be careful in any decision you make because any mistake, she's gone, and you will regret every bit of your actions. The Russians will make you suffer even before they will send us back to the States," James spoke out his mind.

CHAPTER ELEVEN

First Attack

$\mathcal{I}$t was evening. Fred had been doing much body work throughout the day and wouldn't stop thinking about Natasha, who had not even called or shown a sign of being OK. James walked to him. James sighed and spoke out, "Dude, you've been boxing all day. Are you not going to tell me your plans?"

Fred took a break and breathed out. "I feel like tearing Anton down for all his evil deeds."

"You sound funny. Do I hear you saying evildoings? Come on, do you know how many Antons there are in the world? Oh! Simply because you have something in there giving you lots of concern. Why don't you call the police and report the situation to them?" said James.

"Eff the police," Fred replied in anger.

James smiled. "You see, they are all damn connected with the Antons. This is the reason why you have to be careful, because they don't give a damn about your death. Those security men in there are well trained and are twice my height. Look, dude, this isn't your country. Can't you see that? And how are sure that Bogdan can be trusted?"

"What are you trying to say? Bogdan has helped us out in many ways, by mobilizing guys who are going to stand and fight with us, and has also supplied a good amount of guns to us. Do you really want us to leave Natasha and the other innocent people that are caged? Come on, think about it yourself. You don't have to be afraid of this fight, because I know you are stronger and have better tactics than I do in fighting, so you've got to piss it off. Let's show him what we've got. We did this some years back in Miami." said Fred.

"It was years back, a long time ago. Anyway, what are your plans for tonight?" asked James.

"Now you are talking. Come on, let get dressed and proceed to BerryX," said Fred.

"Just like that? Without invitations, dude, I don't think it's gonna work that way. They can't even let us in because they already know about us. They may even end up capturing us," said James.

"The Russians cannot kill us. If they do, you know what it means," said Fred.

James sighed and spoke out, "They could set us up and frame our deaths, and moreover, you are not on a government assignment. You don't even know what we are going to do tonight."

"I have got many plans. If they let us in, we will make trouble and cause a fight so that people could vacate building then we make a hit, but if they refuse us coming in, then we make troubles outside the building, which will also bring more attention and confusion. During these events, Leila could hack into their computer systems because their computer analyst will pay more attention to the present situation. Leila has been looking for possible tactics to distract the BerryX computer analyst, and this plan will help," said Fred.

"Well, not a bad idea. Let's give it a try," James accepted.

Fred and James arrived at BerryX, but the guards refused to let them in. They kept waiting at the door side, where the visitors temporarily stay. One of the security men asked them to leave the premises, but instead they pretended as if they did not understand what he said and stayed around like people looking for someone. Fred's heart was filled with pain and anger as he was strolling around the entrance parameter and it seemed as if one of the guards had just received a call from the inside. The guard walked to Fred, pointing a gun at him to vacate the premises or else he will shoot him. Fred, who had been waiting for this very moment to come, took a little step backward and smartly moved as he collected the gun from him and hit him on the face. The guard fell down unconscious, and other guards rushed toward them, and they began a physical combat. Fred and James were very good in fighting because during their university days, they learned how to fight for self-defense, and in the kind of the work they did, they ought to be strong. When the security guards saw that Fred and James were stronger than them, the security guard that was mostly injured lying on the ground opened fire. Fred and James ran apart to protect themselves behind the cars in the garage. These security men never gave up as they shot, destroying so many cars. When Fred saw that there were many gunshots, he also opened fire, and James joined him. They only aimed at the security's hands or feet; they never shot anyone dead, but they got them wounded. People who were inside the building, the parts of the club where music wasn't played, were already on panic, but the security men kept them calm, that all was well. But the people inside the part of the club where music was being played kept partying because the sound of the music didn't allow them to hear or notice the gunshots outside the building.

James and Fred kept shooting and also destroying things, hoping that the police would arrive sooner, but the police never showed up; instead the guards kept increasing and were now shooting to kill. James rushed to a car, and Fred covered for him. Fred managed to start the car. One of the guards saw him inside the moving car and shot at him and nearly got him. James shot back at him with anger and killed him. Fred rushed into the car, and they drove away with so many gunshots on the car. Some of the security guards immediately entered their cars and started chasing them. Soon the police showed up as they also chased them. James was confused on where to drive to because he didn't drive often on the road like Fred did, and moreover, it was night and the guards' vehicle was close to them already. Fred kept shooting at them as they also did. When the guards' car was very close to theirs, James applied full breaks, letting the guards' car the pass. Now it was them that were chasing the guards, and Fred was able to focus on the shots as he aimed at their fuel tank and the guards' car exploded. When the police that were far away chasing them saw the flames from the exploding car, they called other police to join them, but Fred, who knew the route more than James did, had already handled the stirrings as he began to fire the car like a car racer driving round the city from one street to the other with lots of confusion. And each street he entered, there was always a police vehicle chasing them, and he wouldn't stop because if the police should get them, they would be deported back to America without achieving the goal.

When there was no way out, Fred had to call Jenifer, the computer analyst in his office in Los Angeles, because Leila was busy downloading and hacking through BerryX management's database, so she couldn't help. Fred called Jenifer several times, but she didn't answer. Fred used to be her sex mate, and since he traveled, he had only called her once, and moreover, they had stopped having sex, and Jenifer hated him for that. Jenifer, on the other hand, had never seen Fred calling several times like this before, and when she held the voice message saying "Please call me back, I'm in a big hell," she quickly called back, and luckily for Fred, she was still in the office. Fred sent the navigation of the city to her, and she loaded it in a mainframe computer and began to direct them on what route to take and how to overcome the policemen.

With Jenifer's help, they were able to scale through as Bogdan, who was already tipsy for the day, left the girls he was with and also came helping by assisting with his own car. He asked them to stop their car on a nearby street close to the street where he parked his car and used their feet to locate him with Jenifer's assistance. Fred and James did exactly what he said. So when the police saw the parked car, they never knew what street they entered as Bogdan drove off to the new apartment he had already organized for them because Fred kept him informed.

When they got home, James was very angry. "Fuck, fuck! Damn shit, I nearly got killed! I even killed a man. This is insane. What is this all about? Revenge or justice?" James complained bitterly.

"Blow it off, dude, you did it to protect yourself. It's not intentional. This operation would have been nothing without you. You did well," said Fred.

James, who had already grabbed whisky, spoke out his mind. "I'm not doing this again. It's a mess. Now the police are already looking for us for murder and terrorism. Look, we don't even have any evidence to prove our rights. Then what are we fighting for? How do we get out of this country? It's wild."

Fred, breathing hard and also sipping the whisky, said, "Come on, dude! This is your work. You are a journalist. I thought you were making some documentation on this one?

"What fucking documentation? That I shot someone down and made a car explode? Get up, man I got no four hands. We did all the plans together, and then what time do I have to make documentation? Is it now that I can't even hold my pens? Look, dude, the police will soon get us into custody because we got nowhere to hide. We can't stay indoors all day," said James.

"That is even the more reason why we have to finish this fight. The police are not ready to take this issue to the public. They will keep it hidden, so don't be afraid of them because they want us to go. They can't hurt us. Though they might have some evidence to put guns on our heads, they can't. They just want to protect the image of Don Anton because he's powerful in the state. Can't you see how long it took the police to arrive at BerryX? They never showed up until we drove off, which entails that they are being controlled," said Fred.

"You're right, Fred. You've got to finish this fight because it's the only option. It's enough for the evil men spoiling the image of this country and destroying our future generations. I will keep supporting you guys by supplying constant arms and mobilizing trained guys that will stand and fight with you," Bogdan supported.

James seem tired and weak. "I hope to see this fight end successfully because Ashley won't forgive you if anything goes wrong, and it's really gonna take a longer time for me to forget about it. She is not even answering my calls. Fred, your mum will be very disappointed in you if you fail because you're the only thing she's got left."

"Come on, dude, go take a shower and let go of your worries. Everything is going to be fine. We have succeeded in breaking through their security system, so we can launch an attack at any time both in the institute and even in Anton's house. With the help of Leila and Jenifer, we can do things invisibly. We are really successful today because we have created awareness, and this will be the beginning of his failure. He has to pay for the damages, buy and repair the destroyed cars, and also he's going to lose customers this week for what has happened today. About twenty cars were damaged, and there were no small cars there. They were all expensive cars. Isn't that interesting?" Fred asked.

"Hmm," James sighed. "Interesting, quite interesting, you don't even think about what they are going to do to Natasha, whom you are fighting for. Once they notice that we are behind the attack, of course they should know we are behind it. They will deal with her."

Fred was filled with confusion. "In any case, they are not going to hurt her much because they will still want to keep her beauty, and they still need her. They can only torture her with medical equipment, not physical brutality."

"Hmm! Is that what you think? Are you OK with it? Well, let's hope that all is going to be well with her," said James.

There was pandemonium in BerryX as the security men rescued the guards that were injured and brought them to the medical department in the building. The customers who noticed the fight could not withstand the tension after the environment became quiet. They insisted on coming out of the building. When they came out, they were very disappointed with the situation of things because such thing had never occurred in BerryX. Alexander and other managers tried to calm them down, but some of the men insisted on seeing Anton, who may not have been aware of the situation of things. Alexander gave a guarantee of getting new cars for them or even fixing the damaged ones. He organized private vehicles as the security men drove them to their desired destinations.

Alisa was not aware of what was happening because Alexander had decided to let her out of it. She was busy with her girls, who also did not know what was going on; they were busy entertaining their audience. Natasha had also been stripping all night without knowing the wrongs outside the building. It was just like a joke after her stripping. The guards gently took her to the probation room inside BerryX. She was surprised, confused, and speechless. She wanted to speak with Alexander, but he was nowhere to be found. Alisa had been briefed about the incident, and she was not surprise about it but was angry because Alexander kept her out of the scene. It was a shame for her. She wanted to call Don Anton, but it was too late. There was pressure as everything was put to order and the customers were compensated for their loss and damage. The police secured the parameter, and soon they left. Alexander wanted to be the first to speak with Natasha. When he got a little chance, he immediately went to Natasha speak with her before her torture started.

Alexander walked into the torture room and asked the doctor to excuse him, that he wanted to have a little conversation with her. The torture room was made up of different torture equipment—liquid, solid, and gas—more especially medical equipment. It had been long since Natasha visited this very room, and now she was lying on the bed helplessly, going through torture without knowing her offense. When Alexander walked into the torture room, Natasha was relieved as she sat down, looking at him as if she had never seen him before, with lots of manners.

"You are a disgrace. It's a shame. I'm extremely disappointed in you. Look at what you are doing to yourself because of a mere stranger. I told you to take care of the situation, but it worsened.

I should have never let you go out of this building. Alisa was right," said Alexander.

Natasha was still confused. "What has happened again? It's over between me and Fred, so what else have I done?"

"You will know when Alisa comes to you. I think you can remember her last torture on you. She's really perfect for it, and she's going to get every information out of your head. Fred and his friend were bold enough to attack us on our own premises without fear and have caused a lot of pain and disgrace to the company, all because of you. Our guards were killed, and so many things were destroyed. They are going to pay for the pain and shame they've given to us, and you are going to help us find them." Alexander pointed at her.

Natasha was weeping. "How could they do that? Fred couldn't have done such a thing, and how could I know where they are now? I have been working all night. I never knew what had happened. I have got nothing to do with this. You can have a trace on me or you could ask your security men that have being following me about everywhere I go. I warned Fred to get out of my way. How could they do such a thing?" Natasha seemed worried and at a loss for words.

"Hmm!" he sighed. "You will know where they could be when Alisa comes around with the torture doctor, who will force the truth out from your mouth." Alexander left the room with anger, and Natasha sat back on the bed, crying and confused of everything. It seemed as if the world was coming to an end, and how much she wished to see Fred now, at least to tell him to stay outside, for the company was very wicked and stronger, even more than the way he knew. They were going to make sure that he suffered for the loss.

CHAPTER TWELVE

Happiness and Sadness

$\mathcal{I}$t was 7:00 a.m. Don Anton was feeling the fresh air within his surroundings as he walked around the compound and felt the good things of nature. He beautified his house just like Maxim's house in Russia. It was his dream ever since he had stayed in Maxim's house. He promised himself to decorate his house even better than that of his father's friend Maxim's. He sat down beside the swimming pool, drinking wine and smoking marijuana. Soon his wife, Alina, joined him.

"Good morning, sweet," greeted Alina. She sat on his lap. (Alina still looked very young and attractive even in her early fifties. She was romantic and sexy.)

"Hi, my precious wife. You look so beautiful this morning," Don Anton responded.

She smiled. "It's all for you, my beloved."

"I wonder how life would have been without you. With you, life seems more sweet and special. You are a perfect match for me. No woman could have ever tolerated my behavior and stay with me for this long like you. Without you there would have been no success. It's the reason why I can't hide anything from you." He smiled.

Alina stood up from his lap and took a sip of the wine and kissed him, saying, "I love you more than yesterday." They both smiled and toasted to love and success.

There was a knock on Anton's door, and Alina guessed that it was Nicolas, their son. She quickly grabbed a towel and tied it on her body because she noticed that the door wasn't' locked, and Anton quickly threw his marijuana into the pool. Nicolas ran into the sitting room and didn't see anyone. He quickly rushed to pool because it was Anton's site of relaxation in the morning. He ran to his father's body like they were the best of friends. Anton was very close to his son because he never wanted his son to be treated the way his parents treated him. Even at twelve, Anton still carried him like a baby.

"Oh! Here comes my lovely big boy, Daddy's big friend," said Anton.

"How was your night, baby boy?" Alina asked.

"Fine, Mama!" Nicolas Looked very bad and sad.

"Come on, boy, what's the problem? You look sad," Anton noticed.

"Papa, I told you that I don't like the smell of your marijuana. You've smoked it this morning again," complained Nicolas.

"Come on, boy, Papa is getting old and needs to get rid of some thoughts," said Anton.

"But you promised me that you won't be taking it in the morning but only occasionally. Mama was sick months ago because of excess smoke. I could remember the doctor told her to reduce her smoking and she did, so why can't you stop? Because you told me that marijuana is not good for the body when I told you that when I grow up I will smoke it too." Nicolas was a smart boy. He never hid his feelings from his parents, and that was the reason why Anton must not let him know everything about him. He had always been the best student in his school, and he was not proud of his father's wealth as other kids were of their parents'.

Alina was speechless and later spoke, "It's OK, Nicolas, your papa needs time to quit smoking. It's difficult, and that is the reason why you shouldn't smoke, because it's difficult to stop."

Don Anton smiled. "Your mother is right. Come on, where is your big sister, Victoria?"

"Here she comes," said Nicolas.

Victoria was Nineteen years old, and she was in her final year in the university. She had been begging his father, Anton, to let her travel to London for her master's degree, but Anton would never allow her out of his sight. Anton never wanted to use his ears to hear that Victoria had a boyfriend at her age. He had warned her several times not to have any affair until she was done with her education, but he didn't know that she was secretly having an affair with her classmate Victor, and her mother was aware of it.

"Papa! Papa, good morning. I have brought your phone. It was ringing, and you've got so many voice messages," said Victoria.

"Oh! It's already eight a.m. The phone might have switched on by itself by seven thirty a.m. as I have programmed it. And by the way, where are you going to? You're dressed so romantic, like a girl going on a date. How many times have I told you about short skirts? It's better on jeans trousers. Short skirts are not good for a teenager like you. You could be easily embarrassed by a stupid boy," said her father.

"Sweet, don't say that again. You may hurt her. She's good. I love her dress. It's perfect." Alina kissed her, enfolding her in her arms.

"I know what I'm saying. I could remember when I was a young guy, my friends couldn't set their eyes off a girl that is sexily dressed without having an evil plan," said Anton.

"It's OK. She has a guard monitoring her. She's going to be fine. Let her have fun. So, honey, where are you going to?" asked Alina.

"Mama, you are also asking? I'm very disappointed. Even though Papa may forget that today is my fighting day, you shouldn't have," said Nicolas with anger.

"Ahh! You're right, my son. Today is the final day for the *chaquanda* fight. I hope you're ready for it. You are going to make me proud. You will beat the hell out of your opponent." Anton folded his fingers, demonstrating.

"Yes, Papa, I will win if only you will be there with mama as you have promised, because the last match you were not there, and I wasn't happy with you, though I qualified for the finals."

"I will be there, son. There is still time. I should get prepared," said his father.

Victoria's closest friend, Egine, a beautiful Armenian girl with long hair and who was kindhearted, called her. She was afraid to answer the call in her father's presence because they were going to discuss boyfriend and clothes issues, so she walked far away at the extreme part of the pool to answer the call.

Nicolas thought that she was speaking with her boyfriend. "I hate that boy. I know he's the one calling Victoria."

"What boy are you talking about?" asked Anton.

"Victor, Victoria's boyfriend. Victoria was with him all through last weekend when we went for a walk, and she never gave attention," said Nicolas.

"Come on! Nicolas, what is your business? He's her classmate. Is it bad for you to take a walk with your classmate? Don't be rude to ladies," Alina pledged.

"I do hope that she's got nothing with him, because if I find out that she's having affairs, it won't be easy for her," said Anton.

As they were speaking, the maid called and told them that breakfast was ready. Alina, Nicolas, and Victoria left for dining, and Anton stayed behind, going through the messages and the missed calls. He was totally disappointed and angry about the incident. He called Alexander to set up a conference meeting with all his managers and top security guards, that he was on his way to BerryX to see what had really happened. He also called some of the Mafia that were present in the club to apologize for the misconduct and had promised to replace their cars within the week. It had been a long time since Alina saw her husband, Anton, to be in such anger. Anton left to his company.

At the conference, they narrated everything to him and played the video record of how everything happened. Anton was so mad at them for misconduct and carelessness. He spoke a lot concerning the safety of the clients and concluded by telling them that he wanted Fred and James out of the country within forty-eight hours, or they should get them for him if possible. He also told Alisa to get every information out of Natasha's head and warned that there should be no physical brutality to Natasha because he still needed her service in another branch.

Anton left for his son's fighting competition because he really loved his son and he knew that his son wouldn't be happy with him if he would not watch any of his fights. When he arrived, it was already too late. The fight had already ended, and his son lost.

When Anton left the company, Alisa immediately visited Natasha for the second time with anger. This time around, she came with two guards, whom she instructed to tie her up on the torture chair. They tied her up and left the room. Natasha breathed hard helplessly. "Alisa, why do you so much hate me? I have given you all the information you needed. Why are you still punishing me?"

"Your information didn't work. They have packed out of the apartment. You directed us to the wrong place. It's too bad, and now I have to force you to tell me their new location," said Alisa.

"How on earth would I know?" said Natasha.

"You will know because you did plans together. And this time around, the cameras are off. I can do whatever I want with you. Princess, nobody cares about you now." Alisa laughed and brought out a long string, saying, "This very one will weaken your muscles, and your blood vessels will stop working gradually. So are you are ready to tell me where they are?"

"Go to hell. Go ahead and kill me for nothing. You should be ashamed of yourself for hating me," she cried out. Alisa grew angry and dropped the string and gave her countless slaps until she went unconscious. Alisa was afraid and called the doctor, who quickly put her on medication drips. The doctor told Alisa that Natasha would be conscious, but it may take her hours depending on her strength. Alisa left the room with fear about what she had done.

Natasha was undergoing a trance; she remembered the past when she was still a little baby.

Natasha was such a beautiful little baby. Her parents never played with her because she was the only child. Though her father wanted more babies, her mother never agreed. It was a standard and peaceful home that every man could ever wish to have. Natasha had a little pup that never went out of her sight; even when she was in school, she thought about her pup. She sang and played with the pup every time. The pup was her best friend, and she called her Lucky. Natasha's father, Andrei, was a manager in a private firm. He earned a reasonable income that enabled him to take care of his beloved family. Andrei so much love with his wife, Sasha. Her beauty enticed men. Sasha worked in the French embassy as a translator. She studied international affairs and had learned different languages. Every evening, Andrei and Sasha took their daughter, Natasha, to the city center to ride a horse and play around with her little dog, Lucky. Every weekend, Sasha cooked different types of food, inviting friends and relatives to eat with them. It was really a happy home.

One day, Andrei came back from work weak and confused. Sasha tried to find out what happened, only to find out that her husband had been sacked from work without any settlement or payment. It was really a pity. Months passed by, and he couldn't get any good job, and the house rent had been recently increased. He sold his car for his rent because Sasha insisted that she loved the apartment and didn't want to move to another cheaper apartment because of what his friends were going to say. Sasha's salary wasn't big enough to pay for the rent and to take care of the food. Andrei went through pain, looking at his wife doing all the work he should be doing, like providing for the family and paying all the taxes.

A year later, Andrei's condition became worse. He was forced to change apartments. He moved to a single-room apartment with his family. Sasha wasn't happy about the whole situation. Soon Andrei developed the habit of excess drinking because he had no work. Sasha was not happy with his drinking and misbehavior, so she threatened to divorce or leave him if he continued drinking, but Andrei wouldn't stop. Sasha was sick of the whole situation because they barely had much time for Natasha. Ever since the problem started, so many things had changed. Sasha sought for a transfer in her office, and luckily for her, it was granted. She begged Andrei to leave the city with her to start again, but he refused and wanted to be alone. Sasha couldn't help the situation because he could no longer hear her voice due to frustration. She had to leave with Natasha to another city, but Natasha had also refused to follow her. She said that she wanted to be with her father. Sasha left for another city and left them with no choice.

When Sasha left, life became more difficult for Andrei and Natasha. The little money she gave to Anton to take care of Natasha, he used it for drinking. Natasha herself, as a child, became strong by helping in doing the work that her parents should have been doing for her. She went to school alone, entering the public bus. She was so smart at her age and couldn't allow anyone to cheat on her. All through the winter, she walked on snow every day to school, and she was always late for her class. When her lectures finished, her classmates' parents would come and pick them up while she would walk or go home in the public transportation. It was suffering for a seven-year-old child, who learned everything by herself. Natasha's situation never affected her beauty; instead it nourished her. Sasha, her mother, visited, but she would never speak with her for what she had done. Natasha told her to go away, that she didn't want to see her ever.

Sasha was too proud of her beauty and didn't want to let herself down. She was a high-class woman. Andrei wasn't worth her in any way, not now that he was down, so she left for good.

Life went on with suffering for Natasha until this very day that some strange men came to her father. They confused him and gave him a good amount of money; after all, he was always drunk, so he wouldn't understand what was happening. These men told Andrei that they were from the government, that they were going to train her daughter to be whatever she wanted to be, and he accepted. They came to Natasha and told that they were going to sponsor her in school and universities, that her sufferings were over. Natasha remembered one of the men; she had seen him once or twice in her school premises, and she didn't like the way he was looking at her. She reported to her teacher, but her teacher never understood her. Due to this reason, little Natasha refused to fellow them, but they forced her. She kept crying and screaming "Papa! Do not let them take me away!" But her father was already lost with alcohol and couldn't see. The men injected her with drugs because she was shouting and took her off.

So the company was behind all her mysteries. They were the people that made her father lose his work and placed him in this condition so that they could have her, because if her father were normal, they couldn't dare take her.

When Natasha returned from the trance, she was very angry for what the company had done to her, and now they wanted to finally destroy her life. *It will never happen,"* she consoled herself and pretended to be unconscious.

The police and the guards had being searching all over the city for Fred and James but couldn't see them. The guards had been torturing all the people that they had come across or had a drink with Fred and James.

Days passed by. Fred and James couldn't be found, and the threat to the company increased because no one knew what may come next. Anton was already taking every possible measure to protect his family and his company. He sent his family out of the state to another faraway city, where they could be safe until everything became normal. Thus, he was ready to do anything he wished as far as his family was safe. The company's operation was now limited, and every worker seemed to be alert at all times. Anton had also spent much money in buying new cars for his clients and had made a reunion for their loss. Anton's mind wouldn't be settled until he found Fred and James or until he was sure that they had left the country. He sent delegates to the American embassy and the airport to find out if they were still in the country, but there was no sign of them leaving the country.

Natasha had not been useful to them and refused to speak ever since she became conscious. The doctors tried their possible best to make her speak by using every technique, but nothing ever worked out. Don Anton heard about it and approved that they should use her daughter and make her speak because she was the only thing that she cared for and was ready to die for. The head of the security, Damyan, walked into the probation room to see Natasha for the first time.

Damyan said, "I know it's a surprise to see me here. I would be the last person that you will ever think of seeing concerning this issue at hand." Natasha kept staring at him, and he continued. "I don't know why you have chosen to play it smart. But everything that has a start must also come to an end." He sighed "It has come to my notice that you confessed that you were aware of Fred's plan to destroy the company, and when the company noticed your movement with him, you withdrew from them for your own safety. How interesting could this be? But the tragic part of it is that you are not aware of where they could be. How on earth could I believe you?" He sighed. "I am giving you just twelve hours to think and figure out where they could be. When I come back to this room and you still have nothing to say, then I will order them to torture and kill your daughter. After all, you are of no use to us any longer because the company can never restore their trust in you ever again. They will keep your services indoors until you perish."

Damyan put the child's picture on Natasha's chest and ordered the doctor to release her from the medications so that she could think naturally. Natasha looked at her seven-year-old child and began to cry, begging Damyan not to touch her for she was innocent. Damyan promised not to touch her only if she was able to figure out Fred and James's hideout. Damyan left the room, and Natasha stood up weeping, thinking of how to help with the situation, but the fact remained that she didn't know where they were. Natasha remembered when she last she her daughter, Anastasia, six months ago. Anastasia was very happy and beautiful, and she was growing very fast, smart, and brave. The company allowed Natasha to take walks with her daughter once in a while outside the institute because she was the princess and she deserved some rights. Though she was surrounded by security men, she felt happy being with her daughter. She promised to see her again, and since then she hadn't, and now the company was threatening to kill her helpless little child.

Natasha couldn't stand the thought again. She requested that she make a call to see if she could get Fred on phone. They gave her a phone, and she tried the number several times, but the number wasn't available. Natasha didn't know what to do as time kept running. She disclosed Bogdan, Fred's friend, but the police also couldn't find him. They have searched for him, and there was no trace of his existence. When the time Damyan gave to Natasha finally expired and there was no useful information, Damyan ordered his men to begin torturing Anastasia, and they projected it to Natasha. Natasha cried, begging them to let her speak with the babe, but they refused. Damyan ordered them to kill Anastasia in twelve hours if Natasha would not be able to get real and useful information to them.

Natasha's anger filled up because she couldn't help her own daughter. She left several voice messages to Fred, but none had been replied to, and his line still wasn't available, and time was running faster. She hated Fred for not being there when she needed him most.

Twenty-four hours later, a doctor brought the pictures of how Anastasia was tortured and killed to Natasha for her to feel the pain that Anton was passing through. When Natasha saw it, she wept bitterly and grew wild. She immediately drew out one of the strings and stabbed it on the doctor. When a guard noticed that the doctor was down and couldn't see Natasha, it was too late. Before he could make a move, Natasha drew out his gun and shot him. She also shot down all the security cameras within her vicinity to make sure that they wouldn't know her exact location.

Natasha began to run and continued shooting every security that came her way; she was very perfect in shooting. She never missed. She kept shooting until her bullets were finished, then Alexander, her manager, finally surfaced, and they began a physical combat. Natasha knew all his moves because he was the one that trained and taught her how to fight and defeat her enemies. They fought for several minutes; Natasha defeated him. She tried to call Fred again, and his number went through. Fred immediately showed up with his guys without any hesitation. They had been planning to make the last strike. Some girls who wanted revenge joined Natasha as they all ganged up and brought the company down and set out for the institute, which would be the most difficult place to conquer. They ganged up and used the maps and protocols, and with help of Jenifer and Leila, the computer analysts, they were able to penetrate through the walls of the institute and gave them a surprising package. It was a bloody fight and a gun battle. What the eyes saw was unpleasant. There were many strong security monsters that were perfectly trained for fighting. Fred and James, who had taken much time in retraining their gang, were so confident in them as they fought and killed as many as they could. They freed the entire young students, who surrendered, and also the old students, who gave up in fighting. The labs were destroyed, and the building was set on fire.

The following day, Fred and his gang set out to Anton's house. At their arrival, Anton had already left, but Natasha insisted that the building should be set on fire. James made a report and gathered all his evidence, pictures, and stories concerning the whole incident, which he had been secretly documenting. He passed the matter directly to the court since the police could not take any action. After the first trial, the secret security agency captured Anton and forced him to be judged in the court. At the final trial, he was convicted, detained, and sentenced to twenty years' imprisonment for all his evil deeds. His properties and company was handed over to the government. At the present time, there was change of government, and Anton had not collaborated with them.

Natasha was very happy to see Anton being put to shame but couldn't stop thinking about her lost daughter. She went in search for her father and picked him up from the street, where he begged for food. She cleaned him up but couldn't see her mother before she flew out of the country with Fred to Los Angeles. Anton was transported to a bad prison, where they thought he wouldn't survive. Luckily for him, on getting to the prison, the prisoner guard officer, Arthur, was his classmate in the police academy in Russia. They embraced and greeted each other like in old days. Arthur instructed his boys to take Anton to a safe room and treat him with care.

CHAPTER THIRTEEN

Los Angeles

$\mathcal{F}$red and Natasha were now best friends in Los Angeles. They lived happily and forgot about what happened in the past. Fred wanted to propose Natasha for marriage, but he was waiting for her head to get clear from her past life.

The pressure of friends on Fred to marry Natasha was high because Natasha was pretty, unique, and special, and his friends wanted him to do so before something else came up and he would end up not marrying her after all the stress he passed through. Fred had bought a marriage ring for her for a very long time and had never proposed due to the situation of things. So, a special day came; he decided to piss it off and clear is head once and for all. He flew to New York City with her to visit his favorite hotel, which he hadn't been in for a while. The trip was amazing and crazy. They did a lot of funny things while walking around

New York City because Natasha hadn't been there ever. In the evening, when they came back from the streets, Fred took her to the most amazing place in the hotel for dinner. She really liked the environment and was blushing all through. Fred now gave her a surprise by presenting the marriage ring. To Fred's greatest surprise and dismay, Natasha refused to accept the ring. She told Fred that she still needed time to clear her thoughts and sort some things out. Fred became confused and never knew how much time he could give her any longer. He didn't know what to say again and couldn't read through her thoughts. They had been living together for long time as best friends, happy and enjoying the things of nature, but why didn't she want to marry him? What was he going to tell his coworkers that he has already told about the engagement plans?

Natasha felt very sorry for disappointing and spoiling his day. She tried to cheer him up, assuring him that she would accept the ring when she was ready, that there was no else but him. Natasha really needed to clear her thoughts and be prone to Fred because he didn't know everything about her. Fred never knew that she was using drugs, liquid cocaine, and the drugs controlled her at times; even up to date, she still sneaked around for drugs but had been trying her possible best to put an end to it. She had been hiding this attitude from Fred for a very long time now. Fred couldn't detect it, and even when he suspected, she covered it up with one or two things and wouldn't want to speak or let him come near her. Fred would stay away because he didn't want to hurt her feelings and he knew what she has passed through in life. The worst part of Natasha's life that Fred didn't know about and would feel very disappointed if he found out about was that Natasha once had a secrete affair with his best friend James and still had hidden feelings for him. But James never took the whole thing seriously because he was also under the influence of drugs and felt that he could share the same girl with Fred because they did it to Inna the blond girl.

Natasha's conscience wouldn't stop disturbing her about these very two problems, and she had to address the whole issue to Fred for her to be able to clear her mind and the past.

When they travelled back to Los Angeles, Fred wasn't himself. Natasha could feel it because no man could resist the feeling of the present situation. She narrated the story of how everything started.

There was a day when Fred travelled to another city with Bogdan for some research. That very day, James didn't want to go out. Fortunately for him, Natasha, who thought that Fred was around, came visiting with the intension of having sex with him because she was high on cocaine. James was the only person around, and he was also high on whisky. Natasha was used to the house, so she entered the apartment without even knocking at the door. She wanted to take Fred unaware. She dropped her big handbag in the sitting room and immediately proceeded to the swimming pool to swim away her highness before going to Fred's room, and she thought that Fred was playing a game with James upstairs.

James noticed her presence and came downstairs, staring at her bag; he was about to sense what was in it. He quickly opened her bag, and holy shit, it was coke, which he hadn't taken for a very long time. Without asking, he started snuffing it. He took a lot of it and became excessively high. Natasha came out from the swimming pool, and it seemed as if her highness increased instead of reducing. She quickly rushed to the seating room with her swimming kit. Unfortunately for her, Fred wasn't around. James smiled and admired her half-naked body. He asked her to sit down and she did. He tried asking her questions and how she got the coke, but she couldn't explain. James gave her more coke to snuff, and she couldn't resist because it was like food to her. They were both high, and one or two things led them to having sex.

After that day, it repeated itself again (about three times). Fred never noticed it because he so much trusted James. Natasha liked it because it was really hard sex and she was really satisfied in it. Natasha and James were both lost and were enjoying the highness and the fun in Fred's absence. While Fred was trying to correct Natasha, James in his back was spoiling her more, forgetting that Fred loved her so much. Natasha liked James because James was on drugs with her, but that wouldn't stop her from loving Fred more. Natasha's life was full of confusion. Fred noticed that something was going wrong but couldn't figure it out. He knew that James had changed, but it was normal for James to say the wrong things at times because he drank a lot of alcohol every day at home in the Russian Federation. There was no much workload on him aside from the plan to get Natasha away from BerryX, which took them more weeks than expected.

Natasha was now left in confusion because she was out of drugs and was not feeling normal. She also had a little feeling for James. James, on the other hand, seemed to have forgotten about her ever since they came to the state. He started his normal life, working and doing his normal daily activities, but he was transferred to another company, which made him have less time for himself and friends and fun.

Natasha felt free and released after flashing back, telling the truth about the drugs and her affairs with James, though it was one of the most difficult things that she had ever reviewed in her life, and she was ready to face the penalty. Surprisingly for her, Fred wasn't bothered. He forgave her and also told her about his past, about Inna and other affairs he had while in the Russian Federation. They both promised to change, and she accepted the ring. James was still his best man because he understood everything that happened. James was frustrated because his fiancée broke up with him because of the delay of coming back to the USA from the Russian Federation. Ashley was tired of waiting and couldn't understand what he was doing in Ukraine, and he had told her several times that he was coming soon, but she didn't see him back home and she grew angry, breaking up with him. James was also sanctioned in his office because of his delay in coming back on time, so Fred understood everything and burned the past as they lived with happiness.

Fred married Natasha, and they settled down as couples living in happiness.

CHAPTER FOURTEEN

The Surprise

$\mathcal{T}$en years later, it was announced that Anton had died in prison. When Natasha was told about it, she was very happy but not knew that it was a frame for his escape. Arthur, the prisoner's guard officer, staged his death to let him escape. Anton left the prison and changed his identity and limited his movement as he started his life again, though he had grown very old. Anton, as a brave man, had his plan B for everything he did. He had a secret agency under his command. This agency was the strongest of all. They only took orders from him and no one else. Eleven years ago, when Fred and his friends attacked BerryX the first time, Anton knew that it may not end up well, so he ordered that the smart young student in the institute should be transported to the secret agency, including Anastasia, Natasha's daughter, whose death he framed. When they had the second attack, he ordered that the entire students in the secret agency should be trained as assassins for a future purpose.

Eleven years later, when Anton came out of prison, the children at the secret agency had grown big as higher assassins and had been doing so many nice jobs for their guardian, Denis, who had trained them to be so perfect in killing. Anton paid a visit to them and gave them an assignment, to which he appointed Anastasia the team leader after watching their training.

Anton instructed Anastasia and her team to travel to the United States of America to torture and kill Fred and Natasha. This was the first assignment he offered to them. They must not disappoint him because he was their lord, and he had put his faith in Anastasia, who was quite smart among the six girls. They selected six girls because it would be very difficult to suspect girls.

Anastasia and her team underwent several strong training and lectures and were set for Los Angeles.

Already, when Anastasia was growing up, her guardian poisoned her mind with all sorts of lies, telling her that her mother, Natasha, was picked from up from the street by Anton and he gave her life, protection, and riches but she betrayed him by doing all sorts of odd work. Denis told Anastasia that it was Natasha who killed her father, Vladimir, because she was in love with a foreigner called Fred, and later on, they planned together and attacked the company, the institute, killing so many innocent souls. After the obstruction and havoc, Fred flew out with Natasha to settle in the United States of America. Anastasia grew up to hate Natasha, and now she had been instructed to kill her so she wouldn't look back or even waste time to avenge her late father.

Anastasia and her team set out to Los Angeles in search of Fred and Natasha. The team was very educated in computer systems. They kept searching and hacking into so many computer systems until they got a match for Fred. They started tracing him until they found out where he lived. They also discovered that Natasha had a baby boy that was five years old and she was living very happily with her family. When they reported the situation to Anton, Anton commanded them to kill them all. He wanted to see them die suffering for the pain they have caused him and destroying all that he had taken so many years to build. He wanted revenge by all means because since he came out from prison, he had not set his eyes on his children and he knew that they might have hated him a lot, and if he would go to them, the new government may find out about him being not dead. Anton did not know that his wife, Alina, had died years back as a result of excess smoking and drinking in her past life. She got a heart attack and died instantly. Victoria, his daughter, later travelled to her dream city London. Nicolas stayed back in the Russian Federation, studying in defense academy because his father, Anton, never wanted him to be a military man. Nicolas developed much hatred for his father, even before the announcement of his death, though he knew little about his father's dirty jobs. But the fact that he was convicted made him a crime lord.

Anastasia and her team mapped out on how to get Fred and his family killed. It was a perfect plan because their previous plans never worked out; they wanted the situation wherein Fred and his family would all be at home. In their previous plan, they traced Natasha on her way to pick her son up from school, and when she was driving him back, they wanted to blast the car, but the plan was not perfectly carried out because traffic and other related obstructions. Thus, this time around, they were going to strike at their home. Though their security system was tight, they had no choice. It was in the evening when Fred came back from work and set for dinner with his family. Anastasia and her team sneaked into the compound and quietly disarmed the security men, but one of the security men opened fire and shot one of the girls, and the others grew angry and killed all the security men. Already, Fred and his family, who were seated and eating dinner and cracking jokes, were shocked, when they heard the sound of gunshots. Fred immediately took Natasha and their son, Alex, to a place where he thought they could be safe. He brought out two guns and gave Natasha one. He looked at the security cameras and discovered that none of it was working. He tried calling the police, but the calls couldn't go through because Anastasia's team had used a device to jam all his calls; both home and mobile lines, none could go through. Fred was full of confusion. Soon the team surfaced in his apartment after much struggle with the security doors. When they invaded, Fred used his internal camcorders to monitor their movement, and soon, when one of the girls approached toward him, he shot her down, and unfortunately for him, one of them immediately got him and shot him on his hand close to the chest. He shouted and fell down unconscious. When Natasha noticed that Fred was down, she kept her son safe and sneaked out. Anastasia noticed her movement because she was in the same basement with her, but before she could make any move, Natasha had already shot one of the girls, and just two were left.

Anastasia wanted to make sure that she was the one that would kill Natasha, her mom, because she had taken it as revenge and personal. As team leader, she instructed the last girl to move to another direction while she faces Natasha. When the girl was about to go to that direction, she saw Natasha and wanted to shoot her, but Anastasia shot her down because she wanted to kill Natasha herself. Natasha became confused, wondering why she helped her. Anastasia started moving toward her with anger, and she pulled out her gun, wanting to shoot her. Unfortunately, she wasn't fast enough, and Anastasia hit her down. She stood up and they started fighting. Anastasia was much stronger than her because she was younger and had been trained better. She kept beating Natasha until she was down. It was then that Anastasia now removed her mask so that she would see her face.

A new story began when she saw her daughter. Natasha thought that her daughter had died long time ago. There was no difference between both of them; they were just carbon copies. Natasha started crying and seemed confused, but Anastasia, who had no feelings, told her why she wanted her to see her face before killing her. Natasha began to plead and begged her not to be foolish, that everything that the company told her were lies. Natasha took her time summarizing and explaining the whole story to her and was able to capture her mind. Anastasia started crying and embraced her. Soon little Alex came out from where he was hidden; he rushed to her mom. Natasha told Anastasia that he's her little brother; she embraced him, but the child was afraid of her. Fred, who was unconscious and had missed the whole show, awakened and forced himself to the dining room. When Natasha saw him, she was very happy because she thought that he was dead. They immediately rushed and gave him first aid because he had lost a lot of blood. Anastasia helped to remove the bullet. He was still confused about the whole thing. Natasha called James, and he drove Fred to the hospital. Anastasia and Natasha cleaned the environment and put things in order.

Anton called to know what has happened; Anastasia told him that she had killed them all. Anton insisted on seeing the pictures, but she convinced and told him that the fight was too brutal and there was no time to take pictures, and moreover, she managed to run because the cops came around. Anastasia had now found out everything about her and how Anton had destroyed her mother and everyone that might have cared about her. She flew back to Russia where Anton now lived for revenge. She paid a visit to Anton. She gave him a painful death. She also killed Denis, the guardian, and eliminated every person she ever knew that worked for the company. She also freed the other assassins in bondage.

After her revenge, she travelled to a nearby city to start up a normal life with the intension of working for the government in defense, because she didn't want her power/tactics to be totally useless, and also to help the government fish out the bad leaders in the state.

She went for screening at the ministry of defense, and they offered her a job. Anastasia was happy with a normal life. After a few months, she fell in love with her boss, and in less time, they got married.

It was after few weeks of the marriage that she discovered that she was married to Anton's son, Nicolas. A new story began.

The End